Elizabeth C. Wright

Lichen Tufts

From the Alleghanies

Elizabeth C. Wright

Lichen Tufts
From the Alleghanies

ISBN/EAN: 9783337123253

Printed in Europe, USA, Canada, Australia, Japan

Cover: Foto ©Andreas Hilbeck / pixelio.de

More available books at **www.hansebooks.com**

LICHEN TUFTS.

FROM THE ALLEGHANIES.

BY

Elizabeth C. Wright.

New York:

M. DOOLADY, 49 WALKER STREET.

1860.

R. CRAIGHEAD,
Printer, Stereotyper, and Electrotyper,
Carton Building,
81, 83, and 85 Centre Street.

Somebody says that " A Cathedral would hardly hold my acquaintances—the pulpit would accommodate my friends." This volume, with my compliments, is addressed to the Cathedral full—to the few in the pulpit it is dedicated with the love of

THE AUTHOR.

CONTENTS.

		PAGE
Into the Woods,		9
The Nature Cure.—For the Body,		56
The Nature Cure.—For the Mind,		79
The Perfection of the Natural,		99
A Pilgrim Pagan,		117
A Dream Anthem,		124
The Lost Lake,		127
"Love in a Cottage,"		138
The Dual Spirit,		150
A Word to the Weary,		160
By the Mississippi,		164
Sacrament,		166
Make not Poverty's Cup too Bitter,		167
To-Day,		169
Summer Friendship,		172
By the Sea-Side,		173
I'll tell you, Coz,		175
Pity,		177
Twain,		178
Voices,		180
Beautiful Life,		183
Phantom Building,		185
"Liberty—Equality—Brotherhood,"		187

PAGE

The Picture on the Wall, ... 189
One April Eve, ... 191
By a Lake Side, ... 192
The Death Watch, ... 193
Our own Old Woods, ... : . 195
Snow Song, ... 199
Martha, ... 200
Star-Beams in Shadow Land, ... 201
Stagnation, ... 204
Lullaby, ... 206
Sheaves of Time's Harvest, ... 207
A Voice from Afar, ... 209
Anniversary Letter, ... 211
Anniversary Letter, ... 213
Modern Fairies, ... 216
Fragment, ... 218
Vigil Lessons, ... 219
Life's Nooning Song, ... 221
The Moon of Blossoms in Prairie Land, ... 222
A Reverie, ... 225
Alter Ego, ... 227

LICHEN TUFTS.

INTO THE WOODS.

WE were tired and wanted a holiday, so we went off
into the woods, out of the way of finery and etiquette,
and conventional rubbish, where we should escape from
fashionable twaddle, gossips, and flirts—from humbugs
and household botheration, and be free to rest and
refresh ourselves at leisure. Such an elimination of the
ordinary burden of life's occupations would not only
leave us free, but make us rich with an unheard of
wealth of hours, per diem, at our own disposal.

So running the gauntlet of all manner of croaking
prophecies about colds and rheumatisms, and spiders
crawling into our ears, and caterpillars creeping in at
our mouths, and of all manner of shocked proprieties
wagging dissenting heads at us, and a prospective storm
of " I told you so's!" to hail our disappointed and
untimely return, we packed up our bed and board in
the narrowest possible compass, and went off, like overgrown children, to play in the woods.

This simple performance, like many another, unde-
signedly put a variety of pretty professions to an unex-

pected test of their genuineness. It was surprising to find how many readers of verse, who professed to love poetry, and to appreciate the enthusiasm of the poet-lovers of Nature, shrank from any actual participation in a poetic life. Mr. A., who could quote volumes of poems, thought a man who could live comfortably at home, and have a good hot dinner every day, would be a fool to go into the woods where hard beds and cold dinners would be inevitable.

Then there was gallant Mr. B., who compares women with angels, and grows ecstatic over a fine voice or a graceful carriage, was afraid to trust himself in a camping out excursion "burdened with so many incumbrances!" meaning *ladies.*

Mrs. C., who is fond of Shakspeare, maugre his outlandish heroines in boys' clothes, was shocked at women exposing themselves so, and doing such unladylike things as the ladies of our company proposed to do; and sentimental Miss D. thought it would injure her complexion, and though she could admire Ellen Douglass,

"Though the sun, with ardent frown,
Had slightly tinged her cheek with brown;"

still she feared tan more than she loved sunshine and poetic living.

Mr. E. told eerie stories about belated hunters unwittingly camping on a rattlesnake's den, or at the foot of a panther-haunted tree, or in the favorite retreat of a family of bears, less amiable than those which entertained little Silver Hair in their domicile.

Mrs. F. imagined that there was a tornado somewhere,

keeping on purpose for us, when we should once get
inextricably into the forest, when the tall trees could
come crashing down upon us from every hand; and the
G.'s dreaded wild fire and wilder flood, lost bridges,
unfordable rivers, and nameless disasters. One would
think, if they were to be believed, that our quiet and
"grand old woods" were huge receptacles of dangers
and discomforts, unconquerable and terrific. But some
of us were good woodsmen and knew better, and longed
for the cool pure liberty of their hidden depths.

We were wearied with the experimental rehearsal of
life's drama, and ready to go back of all rehearsals and
acting, into the forests and grottoes where the air
breathes poetry, and all the elements of grander dramas
than ever we have enacted, are created and exhaled by
rock, and tree, and moss—by cool spring and shady
river—by many-toned birds, and bright-hued insects, and
shy wild beasts—by fog, and cloud, and wind, sunshine,
and rain, and dew. We had a mind to lie out under
the skies and catch any divine ideas that might fall, with
falling stars, on the soul not shut in from them by lath
and shingles. We would lie on the bosom of Mother
Earth and listen to her breathing, and thereby interpret
her dreams. We would hush still the life that was in
us, and listen for " the sound of growing things." Perhaps if our own hearts would beat silently awhile, we
might be able to hear the pulses of the green-blooded
plants, and the breathing of leafy lungs. If one of us
should be endowed with genius enough to write out a
faint transcript of the divine poem we found growing
wild in the wilderness, our croaking neighbors would
perhaps shed tears of sentimental rapture over the

beauty of the fragmentary transcript (especially if they did not know who wrote it), although they believed the living poem was not worth taking the trouble of going to see. It was all the pleasanter, however, that they preferred hot coffee and feather beds to cold water and hemlock brush, for we were not in any danger of being crowded or jostled in the Temple of Sylvanus, to which we were going, as devout a caravan of pilgrims as ever visited any shrine.

If we could only have gone as the birds go, unburdened with baggage and unmindful of raiment, we should have been superlatively happy. It was a very great relief, even with these drawbacks, to go where we might wear the same apparel day after day, without remark or change, and this apparel too of the simplest and most convenient character. It would be as incongruous as stupid to carry finery into our democratic woods, where hemlock knots and bramble brush are no respecters of persons, and will tear a dandy's rigging or a fine lady's flounces as placidly as they rend a beggar's rags. I commend you to Allegany underbrush, ye who hate frippery and fandangles, and have a liking for seeing them put to the proof by contact with what is genuine, and strong, and beautiful. But "they that wear soft raiment are in king's houses," or at least far enough from these sombre retreats of verdure; and as the beggars, too, are only to be found in the neighborhood of fine houses, we enjoyed a respite from the heavy presence of both the livers for flattery and the livers on broken victuals.

It is bad enough any time to have some lazy mendicant thrust a lying document under your nose, and

assure you in good fair type that the holder is some
Italian patriot, whose family are waiting in the interior
of Mount Vesuvius for him to collect the means of
having them dug out, and that as he can't speak English
he has to get his begging done by his *printed* paper,
which we all know is but one of a whole edition of such
documents carried about by similar vagabonds. Ten to
one if you tell the scamp he can understand English, he
will swear to you in a most rascally accent, but quite
comprehensible, that he really can't talk at all. But
these poor liars "of the baser sort" are not near so
offensive as many respectable liars we meet every day,
and whose polite falsehoods we dare not kick out of
doors so heartily. When your soul is utterly weary
with shaking hands with pretence, and conversing with
make-believes, you too will be ready for such a plunge
into the wilderness.

A few requisite qualifications were needed, and a few
equipments necessary for our outfit, and though they
were few, they were rare enough to make our party
none of the largest. The members of it must be able
to stand fire and water, and be of sterner stuff than
dolls or carpet knights are made of. It would not do
to have one of us get frightened at a bear track or be
uneasy at sleeping in a wall-less lodge in the wilderness. A love of Nature and Adventure, and an indifference to Luxury, were requisite. These three prime
requisites for an explorer or a hunter, could not be
dispensed with, even for the Lilliputian undertaking we
had in hand.

When equipped we looked a singular group of animals enough. Our captain wore a scarlet upper garment,

called by courtesy a shooting jacket, but which to the
uninitiated bore a decided family resemblance to a red
flannel shirt, fastened by a leather belt buckled around
his waist, and when this was surmounted by his shot
pouch and powder horn, he looked decidedly picturesque,
and would have been gobbled after by all the turkeys in town, if we had been in town. The ladies were
metamorphosed by short dresses, broad hats, and thick
shoes, into as many substantial wood nymphs, ready for
scaling rocks and fording streams.

We left the railroad at Great Valley, for the woods
and river here are still in possession of the aboriginal
inhabitants, the grave and friendly Senecas.

There was an agreeable contrast between the manners
of the white inhabitants around the dépôt, and the red
inhabitants round about. The Yankee curiosity of the
former was all agog to know who we were, and where
we came from, and what we came for, and what could
possess us to do so outlandish a thing. They reminded
one of the comments of the poet Wordsworth's neighbors, who believed his visitors to be a doubtful and
suspicious set of persons, because he and they went "out
o' nights" to enjoy moonlight views.

The Indians, however, to whom camping out was a
more natural phenomenon, and who were not plagued
with so great a desire to meddle with other people's
concerns, took it in a very matter-of-course sort of
fashion, and did not take the trouble to stare after us,
nor to make impertinent inquiries. The courtliest polite-
ness could not have ignored the singularity of our
appearance and proceedings more completely. Much
of the picturesqueness of their character has been civi-

lized away, but the serious dignity and hospitable courtesy remain.

Our first camp was unfortunately chosen, but we
comforted ourselves with the doubtful adage, that "A
bad beginning makes a good ending," and made the
best of it we could. Our Izaak Waltons had a trout
brook down in the programme, and inquired for one at
the dépôt, and a young Seneca accordingly ferried us
over the river, and piloted us a quarter of a mile through
the woods, to a deeply shaded, mossy bank, overlooking
the desired trout fishery. We soon found, however,
that our location was possessed of several qualifications
not down on the programme. The thick damp woods
swarmed with mosquitoes, which invaded even the dense
curtain of smoke we hung to the windward of our
hastily erected tent. We were tired and sleepy, and
having spread a pallet of hemlock boughs we lay down
to rest; but our visitors were hungry, and thirsty, and
importunate, and had greatly the advantage of us in
numbers, and so made our first essay at camping out
rather more spirited and musical than tranquil or
agreeable.

We arose in the morning devoutly thankful that our
ease-loving companions had stayed at home, and sincerely
glad that our camp was easily moved to some more
eligible spot of earth. It was not so easily done, however, but that it might have been a great deal easier
if we had not encumbered ourselves with so much lug-
gage. We had agreed at the outset that we would
take as little as would suffice for our needs during the
expedition; but all being novices at this kind of life, and
some of us having such hospitable ideas of the sufficient,

we found ourselves when all assembled, entrenched
behind a rampart of goods and chattels—provisions,
blankets, artillery, and ammunition—books, portfolios,
and spare garments, so that we felt as "hard set" to
know what to do with our supplies as did the man who
drew an elephant in a lottery. The comforts of life are
very inconvenient travelling companions. How were
we to transport our civilized rubbish through the woods?
If we had been Dutch peasant women, we could have
carried it on our heads, but as our crania had been
accustomed to bear only less material burdens, we had
to cast about us for some different mode of conveyance.
I made "Walden" play Balaam for us, and "curse us"
all that aggregation of the plagues of luxury our own
"cursing" was unequal to.

He says: "The more you have of such things the
poorer you are. Each load looks as if it contained the
contents of a dozen shanties; and if one shanty is poor,
this is a dozen times as poor. Pray, for what do we
move ever but to get rid of our furniture, our *exuviæ ;*
at last to go from this world to another newly furnished,
and leave this to be burned. It is the same as if all these
traps were buckled to a man's belt, and he could not
move over the rough country where our lines are cast
without dragging them,—dragging his trap."—"I think
that the man is at a dead set who has got through a
knot-hole or gateway where his sledge load of furniture
cannot follow him."—"It would surpass the powers of
a well man nowadays to take up his bed and walk, and
I should certainly advise a sick one to lay down his bed
and run. When I have met an immigrant tottering
under a bundle which contained his all—looking like an

enormous wen which had grown out of the nape of his neck—I have pitied him, not because that was his all, but because he had all *that* to carry. If I have got to drag my trap I will take care that it be a light one and do not nip me in a vital part. But perchance it would be wisest never to put one's paw into it."

When we crossed the river to encamp by our trout brook and mosquito factory, we had passed through one of those "knot-holes" where our baggage had to remain behind at the hotel. Now we returned to take up our burdens again and move on.

It was a glorious July day, blue and golden, with the fiery languor of summer's noon, quivering in the heated air, only stirred now and then by a cool breeze winding up the river, like a pure and fresh aspiration in a life of indolence and passion. All day long the active portion of our party had hunted and fished without catching anything, or had romped in the woods and on the river without having the fear of torn garments or wet feet before their eyes. It was utterly delightful to let ourselves loose, and live freely; to have no rules for coming in or going out, for rising up or sitting down; to be emancipated from the bondage of the ceremonial law, and do what pleased us best was paradisiacal enough. The girls tried to learn to throw stones, but did not succeed very well. When the unsuccessful hunters returned, Elvira took a lesson in shooting at a mark. It was awkward business, though she finally succeeded in taking aim, but somehow or other her fingers did not avail to make the thing go off. Two or three attempts failed, and she was on the eve of giving up in despair, when a mosquito settled comfortably on her outstretched

1*

finger, and began to try the flavor of the savory fluids hid under that thin white cuticle.

Elvira is very sensitive on the subject of mosquitoes. She has a great tenderness towards them, and they make strong and lasting impressions upon her. Owing to this amiable weakness she is agitated and alarmed at their approach, and this unexpected salute so startled her that the bitten finger closed convulsively, and the gun was discharged. No doubt the load hit something, for it is not probable that it is yet wandering unresting through the air, but *what* it hit is unknown. Elvira insisted that she fired at the mosquito, and killed it—I, for one, believe her.

Having thus fired our sunset gun, we emigrated from our camp, and pursued our way. Our passage had been secured in a scow, bound for the mouth of the Kenjua, and loaded with provisions. As it was not quite loaded we were obliged to await its completion at the hotel. There was a mingling of odors about the mansion, common about kindred places, and no more disagreeable than at any other time, I suppose; but coming in from the fresh fragrance of the woods, the smells of tobacco and whiskey, onions and pork, soapsuds, codfish, coffee and supper, all united, were disgusting to the last degree, especially to those who could not " eat in faith " in any tavern, because too familiar with the kitchen.

They were a long time loading the boat, and when it was done, they came and told us that one of the hands was too ill to proceed, and that they should not start that night. We held a brief council to discuss the question, " Which shall we do, stay in the inn, or go out of town and encamp?" The "town" was a little

pocket affair, easily got out of, but it was now sunset.
But then July twilights linger longer than most welcome guests do, so that much could be done in that
pleasantest hour of the pleasantest time in all the year.
Susie seemed to have a mind to try the benefit of a
feather bed, but where was the use of coming sixty
miles from our feather beds at home, to sleep in a tavern
where all manner of people sleep? For myself I felt
with a selfish emphasis, that all the sleep in the world
was but of doors, and could be found nowhere else that
night.

I had grown up in woods like these, and they were
home to me. I had been absent from them two years
in the west, and had longed with more unspeakable
homesickness for the evergreen woods and mountain
air, than for home or friends. Among them again I
could not afford to waste an atom of their riches, so
longed for and coveted while I was gone. The mountain echoes were ravishing music to ears wearied with
the flat echoless sounds of prairie land. Who could
afford to sleep indoors and thus lose any part of that
grand Oratorio of unwritten music played by the wind
on a wilderness of harps?

There was a whizzing of car wheels, and a rumbling
of wagons—a clatter of tongues, and the ominous
scraping of a fiddle on the dépôt steps opposite the inn.
There were several young ladies with many-tailed head-
dresses and frightfully big hoops, who were menacingly
polite. These were more to be dreaded than a return
of the ague. The noises jarred harshly on souls longing
for sweet accords and divine harmonies.

A few rods off on either hand, stretching far beyond

our sight, lay the cool, dim forest with its music and its silence whispering together in the twilight. When out of this present little sphere of racket, one could hear the solemn anthem of the far off pines, and the monotonous rush of living waters. Away from this poisoned air, beyond this clang and discord, yet close at hand, a wilderness full of fragrance and music waited for us.

The old boatman, who was an old hunter too, took our baggage and some of us in a skiff, half a mile down the river, and landed us in as beautiful a spot as we could hope to find. Our grizzly and half-tipsy Charon appreciated our errand heartily. He had no wonderment about the oddity of our choice of amusement as our civilized fellow citizens had had. *They* could hardly be convinced that we really meant to do so very odd and uncomfortable a thing as to go out and try to live the poetry which was only fit to read, but the Indians took it as a matter of course, and our boatman delighted in it. He had lived in the woods for many and many a year, he said, and had followed the river until he could pilot it in the dark. We must certainly come to his place on the Kenjua. It was the greatest kind of a place for trout. *Kenjua* was Seneca for *fish creek*, and it was rightly named. He would delight to show us everything, rattlesnakes and all.

We landed on the pebbly beach under a spreading sycamore, which leaned its heavy head waterward, and seemed to be looking at itself in that ever wavering mirror, as it reflected its gleaming white arms and made them sway and beckon upwards, though the tree itself stood still. But the deep water shoaled to a ripple

here, and each separate facet of every wave set up for
a mirror on its own account, reflecting what it could at
a miscellaneous variety of angles of reflection and re-
fraction, so that the sycamore had the pleasure of
beholding its own clearly defined and pointed foliage
run together into an indefinite mop of green, dancing
incessantly on the changeful surface. There was a
curve in the river here like a silver bow, and on the opposite side, which was the outer rim of the crescent, the
water was tranquil as a pond. From its waveless edge
up to the region of clouds, rose the hill abrupt and dark,
clothed to its very summit with an unbroken mass of
evergreens, rising tier on tier up the steep side of this
" mountain wall," whose shadow lay, like a fragment of
midnight, on the pool below. We encamped on the
grass under the lighter foliage of young trees which
clothed our side of the stream. A grassy open space
spread towards the river before us, and a sheltering
thicket gloomed behind. We built three bright drift-
wood fires in a triangle, and within the area we spread
our blankets in gipsy-like groups, and with a roof of
sky and stars above and walls of green tapestry about
us, we lay down, safe and happy, and watched the sparks
fly up like showers of stars among the leaves, and saw
the smoke go rolling upwards like home-brewed clouds,
going to seek their kindred above. A grateful content,
a peaceful rest, such as comes to happy children, settled
upon us like dew upon the grass, and those who did not
sleep lay listening to the " voices of the night."

He who lives under the eaves of the forest will learn
the voices of the trees. They have a definite speech
which the initiated can understand. Here lies the germ

·of truth which makes the charm of the Oriental fable, that some persons can learn the languages of beasts and birds and all living things. Even our dull Western ears can learn, by long listening, to distinguish the differences in the whisperings of trees. If you sit at a street window in one of the thoroughfares of a cosmopolitan city, and listen to the varied gibberish jabbered in the streets, you will soon learn to tell the Irish and Scotch brogues apart, and as easily tell the Swedish from German, or Spanish from Italian or French, without knowing any language but your mother tongue. So in the woods. You may not know what the leaves say in their musical whisperings, but you will know their several tongues. The voices of trees are as characteristic as the voices of the human race. The poet eye of the traveller was in love with the tall tropic palms of the Indian isles, and he thought it would be life enough for a poet to lie ever under that broad, plumy foliage, and be fanned by those leafy wings. But the sea breeze came and whispered, and the harsh, reedy hissing of the palm-tree's greeting disenchanted the finely-attuned ear, and the poet soul returned to its allegiance to the pines of his native hills. We should not have believed him to be a poet if he had not remained loyal to the oldest of the forest kings, and greatest minstrel and bard of them all. The founder of the cone-bearing dynasty lies buried a thousand "aeons" deep under the coal-measures, on the spot where it held up its green æolian harps to catch the primal winds, on which no wings had ever been spread—which had never thrilled to a morning bird's song, nor vibrated to the notes of a grasshopper. The empty sea beat on the desolate shore, and only the lonely shell, and this old Homer of all the trees, heard its throbbing and answered its song. That land has sunk down in the sea, and the waves have rolled over it since then. That ocean has frozen to glaciers and melted again. The land has risen out of its long bath, and been peopled by strange creatures, and that sea has teemed with monstrous shapes, but the cone-trees from the mountains have answered the song of the waves through all the ages and their changes.

Older than man, or beast, or bird—older than the crumbling soil we tread, that has been deposited here, particle by particle, for thousands of years—it stands, sombre and tall, over the deep-buried graves of its primeval kindred, and holds up its æolian harp-strings to the touch of its immortal lover, the wind. Together they chant the heroic song of the Ages, at once a requiem and a battle-cry—a prophecy and a dirge. There is in it a reminiscence of the song of the morning stars when they sang together—a lingering echo of the great shout of joy over the new creation, uttered by the sons of God; and the dying sigh of the dead Ages and their lost types of being, is repeated in the song of the Pine.

A stranger would hardly know the roar of the wind among the hemlocks from the deeper and hollower sound it brings out of the longer leaved tops of the pines, but a novice could distinguish the difference in their whispers. It is the difference between a robin's "Good morning!" and the wood-thrush's "Good night!"

There are two kinds of aspen trees here in the under-wood, distinguishable from all other trees by the fairy

tap, tap, tapping of their leaves against each other when
the other woods are still. I know no common names by
which to distinguish one from another. They are both
known hereabouts by the names of " Popple," " Quak-
ing Asp," and " Aspen." The *tremulöides* is the more
restless and sensitive of the two, as well as the more
graceful. Its smooth, heart-shaped leaves dance on
their long flattened stems long after the wind has gone
by, and by the constant beckoning of its many hands
seems calling the rover back again. A sound like the
clapping of elfin hands issues from it, and seems to be
calling the invisible air with an oft-reiterated " Come !
Come! Come!" The more sleepy *grandidentata*, which
rolls its fuzzy leaves out of its white buds a fortnight
later in the spring than its early rising relative, is a
slightly graver personage, and does its tap-tapping to
a slower tune. Its leaves dance, but in a more solemn,
or mayhap a lazier measure, for it is not always easy
to tell laziness and drawl from gravity and solemnity.
The grandiose name of the larger aspen, however, im-
presses one with the notion that the rapidity of the
movements of the *tremulöides* would be beneath its
dignity.

The magnificent magnolia acuminata of the Alleganies, known by the stupid name of cucumber tree,
shudders audibly when struck by the wind. It is a
grand and peculiar tree, well nigh as conspicuous in its
individuality as the pine. Taller than any neighboring
deciduous tree, it lifts its top straight above its com-
peers, and even its branches and lesser boughs follow
the proud aspirations of the trunk, and lift themselves,
massive and angular, right upward at the ends. There

is no pliant swaying, no graceful drooping of outermost twigs or pendant foliage, but all are as upright as a Prussian regiment or a Puritan Sunday school. It is against its nature to bend, and the hoarse shuddering sigh with which it meets and buffets the blast, is uttered by no other tree. Its great oval, spice-breathing leaves carry off the wind in spouts, like a multitude of eaves troughs slanting to the leeward, and the rushing of these divided currents has the disturbed and warlike tone of opposing forces. It affects one like a remembered trumpet blast.

Then there is the birch. It grows to a great tree here on the Alleganies, and has an elm-like foliage, and an odor of winter-green. I cannot describe its voice, for it is to me so associated with a very different sound, that I cannot think of them separately, though they are not alike in the least. In our old sugar bush there used to be a great black birch which had many years agone taken root on a fallen log, and its long roots had run down on either side to the earth and taken fast hold there while the fallen tree decayed away from beneath it, leaving our birch standing on a five-legged stool of its own twisted roots, in the air. Another fallen log lay near by, covered with a thick mat of yellow, feather-like mosses, and on this used to stand a patriarch grouse, or " pheasant," or " partridge," as he was called, and wake the dreamy echoes with his drumming. We very rarely saw him, for he was a shy bird, but we heard him many times a day in his season, and found his tracks there. We children used to tap the old birch and catch its profuse sweetish sap in a little trough, to drink of its diluted spicery ; and that draught and its neighborhood, and the tremulous thunder of the grouse's wings, with the hum of the wild bees which used to drink at the same place, are all called up by the birch's voice, and become part and parcel of it, past the power of analysis to separate them.

No more can I remember the voice of the maple without the crackling of the fire and the singing of the heating sap-kettles, and the tinkling drip of the drops from the trees into the receivers all being mingled with it. Nor has memory any language for the sycamore unassociated with the dash of rippling waters. It is not to be regretted, however, for such associations make much of the poetry of the unwritten language of trees. Would you wish to forget in connexion with the long drawn "Hush-sh-sh!" of the willows by the stream, the plunging sound of the musk-rat as it leaped from its perch on shore and swam to a place of obscurer safety? Or could you afford to drop out the sound of the occasional leaping of a fish from its element, to seize a passing fly; or the creaking whiz of a dragon-fly's wings, as it darted to and fro. Would you like to remember the beech or oak without the squirrel with puffed cheeks, crying "chip! chip! chirrrrr!" at you, as you tried to measure the measureless "O o o o o o o o!" sung by the wind in the tree tops?

You might as well try to think of a sleeping village without its barking watch-dogs guarding it, or remember

"Yon ivy-mantled tower,"

without thinking of its moping owl, "complaining to the moon."

There is a language too, which is not spoken by the voice, but uttered in look, or motion, or taste, or odor. The resinous smell of the coniferæ speaks as distinctly as their wind-swept leaves. The penetrating, disease-dispelling odors of tar and turpentine, rosin and balsam, have the same primeval reminiscences as the voices of the trees that produce them. They suggest questions concerning the probability of some post-alluvian beauty decorating herself with beads of fossil rosin, as the belles of our day wear ornaments of amber. They may guess of the rosin, as we guess of the amber, how it was distilled in the laboratory of the sea-loving cone tree's trunk in some unknown ante-human era. The bitter spice of the magnolia and tulip trees tastes and smells so suggestively, as though they had had human experiences, that we wonder if those trees never travelled, nor loved, nor hated, nor suffered, nor enjoyed like us.

When we read of birch and willow twigs being found undigested in the stomach of a fossil mammoth, we wonder if some birch-eating school-boy's fossil remains might not suggest to the post-alluvians, the notion that the genus boy was birchivorous in its habits. We alluvians would be more apt to class the pedagogue there, but geology would hardly teach so much to the scientific of the next era.

There is an odor of antiquity about the birch and such trees as are found as fossils, though it is but a mediæval sort of antiquity after all; its ancientness toned down and mellowed by the far older and darker background of the cone-bearing ages that came before. This sort of reflection and research is the preparatory course of study needed in order to understand the language of trees. *These* dead languages are super-classical, and have the advantage of being real knowledge and living poetry, beside the discipline and dead lumber which are the recommendations of the mere dead *human* languages.

Within the sphere of purely human oldness there are some trees and herbs geologically both ancient and modern, which are venerably hoary with the rime of the winters of many generations of men. The cedars of Lebanon would seem as old as Lebanon itself to our thoughts, and as venerable as the temple of Solomon, and as mysterious as Masonic rites, even if we knew nothing of the story of its fossil kindred. And to those who, as children, took the oar-like seeds of the ash, and hung them to the lip of the cypripedium, the " whippoor-will's shoe " of the Senecas, and called them the oars of a fairy-boat, the ash becomes an ancient and legendary tree, even before they come in after years to read the story of the evergreen ash tree yggdrasill, whose roots the dragon Niddhögg gnawed, and whose branches sheltered the Norns. Those fairy oars have rowed that legend through the age of fable down to the matter-of-fact sea of modern literature, and yet not a vein of that charmed tissue is broken, and the sharp lamina of the blade is as delicately veined and nerved as in the days when the Eddas were new. The mystic ceremonies of the Druids stick to the viscid berries of the sacred mistletoe, and something of the smoke of their altars lingers in the scent of the oak on which it grew.

But these legendary reminiscences are only historical, and not the natural language of the trees themselves.

They speak of them only to those who know the story, but never tell the stories themselves even to the most intimate of their acquaintances. They are no part of the tree history proper, only an episode in which there is more of the history of men than of trees, and we cannot expect trees to learn a new dialect to add to their speech, that they may be able to prate of men. Yet we, being human, like this odor of old human ideas clinging to them, and would willingly interpret their speech awry in order to find our fore-fellows mentioned in their chronicles.

The less pretentious herbs of the field and forest have a language as pithy and vigorous, according to their kind, as the utterances of the lordlier trees, but it is no such "language" as the plants are accused of in your "Flora's Lexicons" and "Flora's Interpreters."

Imagine Flora treading on the margin of vanishing winter snows, leaving flowers behind her for footprints, and beckoning the leaves out of their buds, and the flowers from their occult hiding-places, with her floating garments and drooping garlands, wearying her wreathed arms by lugging around an eight-cornered dictionary, and attended by an ominous interpreter tagging at her heels! Bah!

This sentimental flummery could no more be mistaken for the "language of flowers" by anybody who had ever heard the real language, than the quizzing schoolboy's "Iggery, wiggery, foggery, youggery!" could be mistaken for classic Latin by a Cambridge Professor.

But it is surprising how many people take such stuff for poetry. It seems to be taken for granted that every-

body who likes poetry or flowers must be maudlin
enough to like these satiny, perfumed, illustrated books,
with a flower's name in two or three languages (and not
always correct at that) at the top of the page, and
selected fragments of the productions of poets and
poetasters strewed down the space below the name and
motto.

We even find a few pages at the end of our Botanical
text books devoted to this twaddle, and when the books
have been used awhile we find these pages have been
used more than any other, the leaves falling apart quite
naturally at the silliest places.

One of these vapid prettinesses, designed for sentimental young girls to read, is entitled the "Floral Diadem," though poor Flora must be as mad as King Lear
before she will wear such a ridiculous diadem over her
"ambrosial locks." This book, like its congeners, makes
some botanical professions. One of the first articles in
it contains the following erudite morsels. "It (the
Spring Beauty) appears in the verdant meadows, upon
the grassy hills, and in the shady groves, lifting its pink
striped blossoms above the ground. *It varies in color
from sky blue (!!) to a fair white (!!)*. But by far the
most common and the most beautiful are the variegated
ones, delicately striped with pink and white. It is one
of the earliest and loveliest flowers of spring, and *is
known by the proper name of Houstonia (!)* but its
more common and pretty name among our young flower
gatherers is *Spring beauty (!!)* and from its nature and
appearance is frequently called *Innocence (!!!)*" Did anybody ever print three more ludicrous blunders in one
sentence ? No country girl of ten years old would

mistake the Innocence for the Spring Beauty. You could as easily make her believe a peony to be a rose. They are about as much alike as a tulip and a daffodil. Yet the astute writer describes *both* flowers without discovering the difference, even quoting the verse,

> " It comes when wakes the pleasant spring,
>   When first the earth is green,
> *Four white and pale blue leaves it has*
>   *With yellow heart between !* "

and does not discover that though it describes the Innocence, it does not count straight nor paint right for the Spring Beauty or *Claytonia* (instead of Houstonia), which has *five* red and white petals *always*.

Again hear the astounding discovery made by this discriminating naturalist. " It opens its bright blossoms in the evening, and continues until late in the morning, and then closes them during the rest of the day." As neither the Houstonia nor Claytonia answers to that impeachment, doubtless the Primrose or Morning Glory was also confounded with them in the author's mind. But hear now! Here come the " ginniwine scientifikils."

" Well do I remember on a fair day in spring, taking my botany book and going to the grove to gather and analyse the wild flowers that there bespotted the quiet landscape. This (which ?) is the first I plucked by my path, whose history I traced and whose name I learned."

And the *last*, I should think, by the accuracy displayed in distinguishing family differences in plants. The two or three thus amalgamated in this floral olla podrida do not belong to the same species, genus, or natural order—

are totally dissimilar in roots, tops, leaves, stems, flowers, and seed; not even being of the same color or manner of growth, nor the same size, the Spring Beauty being thrice the diminutive dimensions of the other, and growing scattered about everywhere, while the Innocence grows in patches, making a regular little sod of its own. So much for sentimental botany sweetened with the "Language of flowers." If the Diadem's piety, which it professes to teach, is as bogus as its botany, we wish it a speedy death, and a funeral sermon as profound as its own scientific researches; and would suggest as a text the one found on the 47th page of the Diadem, but *not* in the Bible:—"Consider the lilies of the field, they sew not, neither do they spin!"

If these books, and the counterfeit "language" they teach, had not usurped the place of the beautiful science on which they have grown like parasites, they would not be worth the trouble of chastising. But when sensible people come to the conclusion that botany amounts to little more than the language of flowers, and that language such idiotic gibberish as I have quoted from, surely it is time to enter a protest against such usurpation and desecration.

No! Ivy does *not* say "Festivity," nor "we will not part!" as these Lexicons tell us, but it says "Old ruins —crumbling walls—and churchyard stones!" and suggests bats and owls.

To a sentimentalist of this sort, laurel will say "Glory" according to the books, while to the farmer it more emphatically says only "Dead sheep!" Yet there is hardly a bumpkin in all the woods who does not pause to admire the laurels when they are in bloom. It matters nothing to him that it is not laurel at all, but masque-rading in a borrowed name. It is just as beautiful as though it were a true laurel and did not kill sheep. I once heard a drunken and stupid stage driver wax eloquent in describing the June dress of a thirty mile laurel patch he was driving through, between the Susquehanna and Allegany rivers. It was mid Novem-ber, but the woods were green with the vivid verdure of the undergrowth of Kalmias, and the duskier over-growth of pines.

"It's jest a fair *sight* in June!" he said, "jest a great posy bed all the way. There ain't no garden like it. All the roses in Pennsylvany ain't a primin' to it, I tell *you!* Jest come here in June, and you'll say you never saw flowers afore!"

But then he digressed immediately from the beautiful to the murderous, to tell how deer sometimes got caught by the horns in the laurel brush, and became an easy prey to hunters or wolves.

Doubtless the laurel, like everything else, varies its speech to suit the notions of its listener. To me the laurel speaks less of glory, or murder, or beauty, than of liberty. It is untamably wild. Try to cultivate it, and it dies. Leave it in its native haunts, or cultivate around it, even if you do not touch it, and it dies. Transplant it ever so carefully, into a place apparently every way congenial to it, and it grows no more. The only con-dition you can supply to make it thrive, is absolute liberty. Let it alone, and make everything else do like-wise, and it thrives. Meddle with it, and it dies. This is emphatic language, and yet no sentimentalist sets down "Liberty or Death!" as the motto of the Kalmia. I see

in the Horticultural books, ways laid down for the cultivation of this shrub, but I never knew one to succeed
in raising them, though I have known many to try.
Many of the orchidaceæ have this same deadly antipathy
to civilization, and can only be enjoyed by the human
race in the place where nature puts them. Do but
loosen the earth about their roots, and the fibres begin
to shrink and wither. Their strange fantastic flowers
wilt away, and the buds blight. They say very plainly,
though not loudly, " Mind your own business!" and if
we disregard the admonition, they die to rid themselves
of our meddlesome impertinence. Yet, as they are very
charming, unobtrusive flowers, a sentimentalist, if he
interpreted them at all, would make them say, "Shrink-
ing timidity," or some other such twaddle, if he did not
ignore these characteristics altogether, and give them
some absurdly incongruous speech to make, as if some
nine years' old urchin in short jacket should set about
making Mark Antony's oration over the body of
Cæsar.

There is no richer native order in the Northern States
than the Ericaceæ, and none with a more classic-like
mellowness of language. Abounding in graceful and
varnished evergreens, in aromatic and spicy bitters, and
tenderly colored and fragrant flowers, it has a fuller
vocabulary and a more flexible tongue than most vegetable tribes possess. I have already interpreted the
speech of the Kalmia, so far as I understand it, but how
differently speaks the wonderfully fragrant flowers of
the leafless Azalea. It has no winter-loving foliage, to
glitter through the drifting snows, or to welcome the
caresses of the north wind, but an affluence of deep rosy

cups for the bouquets of spring. It comes just after the
rock-loving "Arbutus" trails its garlands among the
dead last year's leaves, over the sunny side of wooded
hills, breathing out its odorous life in incense. Just
now, in mid July, one of the smallest and prettiest of the
tribe, the pipsissawa or prince's pine, is in its glory; its
sharply notched, deeply veined, glossy evergreen leaves
making a background which throws its clustered, rosy,
waxen bells, or rather Lilliputian saucers, into exquisite
relief above.

These each have a speech of their own; each dainty,
exquisite, and ambrosial, but different and individual
enough. The Azalea gives one an impression of fragi-
lity quite foreign to the other two. It is a banquet
flower, enjoying to the full what it has to-day, and is
nothing to-morrow. It says, "Let us eat and drink, for
to-morrow we die!" The trailing arbutus says as
plainly through the invisible sources of its fragrance,
"Seek and ye shall find!" The pipsissawa crowns itself
with flowers at midsummer, and, like Barnaby Rudge's
raven, cries "Never say die!" to everybody who will
listen. There are multitudes of carefully cultivated ex-
otics not half so beautiful or piquant as this wild flower,
that half our florists have never seen. The plant is well
known to empirics as a medicine, and to garland makers,
at Christmas, as a beautiful decoration, but who expects
it to bloom, or who has seen its flowers? The somewhat
similar, but not half so pretty, wintergreen, is a very
attractive plant to children where it grows, not only the
spicy scarlet berries but the entire young plant being
eaten by them. One hardly expects eatables to speak
to the eater in any but gustatory language, yet it is a

significant fact that the tongue is both the organ of taste and of speech.

Many persons having a vague understanding of these vegetable languages, and feeling their unwritten poetry quivering like music through their souls, imagine that any scientific knowledge of plants would dispel the poetic afflatus, distilled like an etherial essence in the hidden nectaries of flowers, and the secret chambers that brew the volatile oils. They are afraid of being disenchanted by huge words, and disillusions by prosaic facts. I fancy those persons would prefer music to be sung in a foreign language, so that the effect of the sound need not be disturbed by a comprehension of the words.

There are a class of botanists of the mechanical sort, who are to science what the patent-note singing books are to music—mechanical, soulless anatomists of parts, and dictionary-like vocabularies of technology, who perceive no laws, conceive of no causes nor forces not laid down in the text-books: mere shallow smatterers and quacks, who look at a plant as they would at a new chimney, to see how it is built, and when its external structure is discovered, and its habitat indicated by a vegetable directory, and its name and lineage discovered in unintelligible Anglo-Græco-Latin, are satisfied, especially if its chemical qualities recommend it to the cook or the physician. These scientific bores disgust those who *love* flowers and trees for the sake of their beauty and poetry; and so, because some scientific prattlers are stupid and prosy, they think that the science of plants itself is unlovely and undesirable.

If our only conception of artistic music were the thrumming of a novice on some tormented and wailing piano, we should hate the name of musical art, and feel the very calling it music took some of the sweetness out of the unwritten music of nature. But if no tyro ever drummed discord on a piano, no Thalberg ever would have drawn divine harmony from its keys. We must have some prophetic notion of the end from the beginning, in order to make the beginning endurable. Many would-be musicians never get beyond the dreary regions of thumped and rattling keys; but there are a few who reach that region where Orpheus dwelt, and move the hills themselves with the utterance of their melodies. There must be beginners in everything; but should the ignorance of beginners frighten off or disgust the lovers of truth and nature from the science which is a key to both? There is a world of difference between using a dictionary to find the meaning of words, and hunting up words on purpose to find them in the dictionary; and that is the difference between the quack naturalist and the real one. The true lover of poetry, when reading some soul-stirring poem, may come to a strange word, and not find the poem lose its significance and beauty if he should refer to a lexicon for the mean-ing of the new expression. A pedant may read a work on purpose to mouth its most obscure phrases, after he has hunted out their meaning in a vocabulary. So a true naturalist will find many hard words in the beautiful poem of Nature, and will search out their meanings, not for the love of *words*, but for the love of *meanings ;* while the quack will swallow the technical glossary for the sake of putting it forth by mouthfuls. But we need not let that spoil nature for us, nor need those whose ears are attuned to the sweet accords of the speech of growing things allow these pedantic and sentimental "Flora's Lexicons" to prevent us from learning, at first hand, the real "language of flowers."

This night might have been taken for an ideal model of one for "camping out." The soft breeze which wound up the river dispelled the mosquitoes which so tormented us the night before, and yet scarce broke the deep hush of midnight by its faint and drowsy breathing. Our mother was very near us then—nearer than we can ever approach her by daylight. Her breath breathed into our nostrils. The slow pulses from her deep fountained vital currents throbbed in our arteries, and her life became our life. Thank God! for the taintless highland air that made such a bivouac safe, even for those who had never tried it before!

But even the keen relish of a new experience could not long keep awake a weary crew, who knew that after that night's lullaby was over a new day with new experiences would call them to action again. Before day began to be visible to our eyes the wood-thrushes, who slept nearer the sky than we, began to break the silence with their gushing songs. Shade after shade of darkness ebbed away before the dawn, till at last a golden glory crowned the hill tops, and showed them not so far off as they seemed in the sombre twilight of the evening. How near the sky itself looked here! Only a pine's length above the taller tree tops. The white fragments of cloud that floated between the sky and hills seemed in danger of tearing their silvery robes on the loftiest branches, and the wide-winged hawk that sailed among them, bathed in them without going beyond our sight. The sky looks immensely farther off from the open country, and the clouds are miles away. They are both too far off for neighbors and friends, such as they are to the highlanders. Here morning did not seem to flame upon us from a distant pavilion, but arose melodiously from some breezy couch among the eastern hills, and, shaking out a thousand perfumes from her dew-dropping locks, smiled on our camp and kissed us.

We arose and trimmed ourselves, and ate our breakfasts, and chattered and sang, like the other happy creatures about us. Morning is the time to laugh and be glad, as evening is the time to muse and be serenely happy; so, as we had ended one day naturally, we began the next naturally also, and laughed and were glad.

The promised boat came early, but we were ready and waiting, and embarked for the regions below with alacrity and glowing expectations. We neither rowed nor sailed, but were drifted and *poled* along, seated upon perches like so many turkeys gone to roost, on as many flour barrels cushioned with our own bedding. The boat was a scow—a sort of shallow, square contrivance for carrying loads, and this was loaded heavily. The draught was very inconsiderable, but the channel of the stream on the ripples was more trifling still, and we accordingly stuck fast several times. When stuck only at one end, we all went to the other extremity of the boat, and thus lightening that part, floated off again; but when hung by the middle, that kind of tactics would not do. Overboard went a lot of bipeds into the warm flashing water, and seizing the four corners of the craft with vigorous hands, and applying strong shoulders to them, swung the great thing, thus lightened

and urged, around broadside to the current, and free
again. In again leaped passengers and crew with a
joyful burst of congratulations, and a considerable extent of dripping garments to be again hung over the
sides of those barrels to dry in the wind and sun. Perhaps the soaked individuals within them tempted a siege
of rheumatism or pneumonia by their many wettings,
but no such distress came in consequence.

We had deep water, and slow, dream-like floating on
a mill pond up to the dam, which was high and had the
"slash" on besides, and was consequently impassable.
A delay of several hours occurred here, as the boat had
to be unloaded, and taken around the island, which
formed one shore of the pond, and floated and dragged
through the narrow and shallow channel on the other
side, and reloaded at the foot of the dam. Unloading
our own trumpery and piling it up for reloading, we
proceeded down the river on foot. There was a house
here in the process of erection, and loitering behind my
companions, in a deep hollow, to examine some plants, I
became the unintentional repository of a confab among
the carpenters, as to whether we were Chinese, gipsies,
or other outlandish folk ; but having secured the dalibar-
das I was in search of, I emerged from my hole
and lost the conclusion of the matter, but went on,
mentally resolving that as we would not be Chinamen
on any terms we must be gipsies, and might as well go
to fortune-telling at once.

The river banks are high and steep, and often nearly
perpendicular, with a gravelly beach at the foot at low
water. Along this gravelly river's margin are sprinkled
many cold clear springs of water, close to the river's

edge. A slight freshet covers them all with turbid
water from the hills and surrounding country, but now
that the river was low and warm, these beautiful little wells
we scooped out with our hands to make drinking places,
were an overflowing blessing to the thirsty. The banks
were covered with uncivilized verdure very delightful to
rummage amongst. Ripening whortleberries made a blue
glimmer among the sparse and patchy foliage of the low
undershrub which bore them, both making a harmonious
picture on the russet hemlock " muck " in which they
grew. The chestnuts were in full bloom, and no pity
for nutless squirrels next fall deterred us from adding
some of the longest and most graceful of their plumy
flowers to our collections. Diervillas out of their common yellow uniform, sported lively orange red blossoms
on the steep declivities. Two dainty species of Apocy-
num spread their delicate foliage and pink blossoms over
the hot sand, and among the duskier greenery above.
The ragged border of hemlocks fringing the top of the
bank bounded our horizon when we were down by the
water, but narrow as our range of vision was there was
plenty to see. The spring flood-tide of bloom was over,
as well as the fullest flush of the summer flowers, but
enough yet blossomed to reward research and continually whet our appetites for more. The seed growth
of the deep-woods plants, too, was a continual feast of
discovery to most of us. Having spent in woods
like these more summers than I care to count just
now, this forest growth was well nigh as familiar as
the foliage in a kitchen garden; and a two years' resi-
dence in prairie land had made me hunger and thirst
for these woods and waters so keenly that I went

2*

"maundering" about, greeting my old friends beside every log and under every bank. They made fun of me, and dubbed me the "Dictionary" that day for the unconscious pedantry of mouthing so many jaw-breaking names for innocent little weeds, which were wholly unknown to the Greeks whose language has been appropriated so much in naming them. These hideous names, which serve as so many scarecrows to frighten off lazy schoolboys and girls from this most beautiful study the green Earth affords, have become as pleasant as household words to me, from constant use. In order to learn them, I contracted a habit of talking to plants in my solitary walks, and calling them by these names, and, despite the absurdity of the thing, I continually betrayed this habit among my fellow travellers; so I was the "Dictionary." Ah, well! one could be much worse a book, if not a less poetical one.

Elvira took a second lesson in shooting to-day, and so far improved upon her practice at the mosquito hunt of the day before, that she brought down a woodpecker from the top of a hemlock, much to her own astonishment.

When the boat landed us on the right bank of the stream a few miles below, it was at one of those riverside fountains which gushed out in the shade of a green though fallen tree, which was bathing its head, with its "terms inverted," in the Allegany. Near this the Indians had made a footing in the precipitous bank, up which we climbed, and after a half hour's reconnoitring, selected a spot overlooking the river, and went to building our camp. We encamped under a beech tree, using a stout horizontal limb, which stretched towards the river, for the ridge pole of our wigwam, supporting its outer end with a stake. Against this ridge pole we leaned boards and slabs, which were plentiful in this vicinity, and here we had a picturesque camp, opening riverward and commanding a prospect so lovely in its rural simplicity and quiet that our artist took possession of it immediately. We were on the outside of a curve, just above Jemmison's Bend, and could see a long panorama of inverted hills and woods done in crystal far up and down the "Beautiful River"—for the Senecas continue the name Ohio, or rather Ohe-yu, or "Beautiful River," up to the very head of the Allegany, which is a name they never applied to the river.

I have heard, though I do not know on what authority, that Allegany signifies "Head of the mighty." If it does, it is in allusion to the mountains of that name, from which so many rivers rise.

The river near our camp afforded us a delightful opportunity for swimming and playing in the water—a pastime never out of date—an enjoyment new every summer. The Seneca children seemed to be amphibious, as though they were akin to porpoises. One little fellow played riding on horseback, by sitting astride a floating slab and propelling it with his feet.

A descendant of Mary Jemmison, the "white woman," lived a quarter of a mile off, across the river, and his family crossed the river in a log canoe, which lay at the landing, several times a day, to get cold drinking water at the spring under our bank. A woman with two children came oftenest; and it was a marvellous sight to see her send that narrow craft as straight as an arrow across the rapid stream. She used a setting pole, and stood up in the middle of the canoe, and would give it such an impetus before it reached the deep channel where her pole was too short to touch bottom, that it would dart across the swift current without perceptibly swerving in its course. The gentlemen of our party tried to learn the trick, but bungled and failed every time, to the great amusement of the skilful boatwoman, whose clear musical laugh it was worth being laughed at to hear.

The next day was Saturday, and as we had a written invitation to a grand Sabbath-School picnic a few miles down the river, our company gladly availed themselves of the opportunity of seeing the people together.

The old rulership of the chiefs is superseded by a republican form of government, and the picturesqueness of manner and attire are passing away. They are obliged to be civilized in self-defence. If the white people about them were not the most barbarous of their race, the Indians would probably prize civilization more. As it is, the exemplifications of enlightenment they are in the habit of associating with, are not such as present very powerful attractions to an unvitiated taste. At a world's fair of scalliwags, I think some of the white scamps on the river in the Reservation would take the premium for being the most worthless, drunken, foul-mouthed blackguards possible to find. Added to this chronic nuisance which empties itself into the river from Ellicottville and the other towns near the Reservation, especially on Sundays, to fish and play the ruffian or ribald clown generally, there is a periodical nuisance of a more business-like and less idle character, but which is morally no better for the Senecas. All the up-river lumber region uses the river for a market road, and whenever there is a freshet of sufficient magnitude to make the stream navigable for rafts, which happens twice or thrice a year, the region below is deluged with lumbermen, who at home are not generally the best possible specimens of Christian civilization, but who leave their greatest stock of good behavior at home when they go down the river. They are oftener than otherwise rough, profane, and drunken. Now the railroad, with its degraded hangers-on, crosses the Reservation, and runs near it for many miles. There are, however, some permanent residents not to be reckoned in this category. On asking a Seneca if our baggage would be safe alone at our camp, he said, "I am afraid not. The Indians and the neighbors (the white residents just mentioned) won't touch any thing, but there are some Irishmen and white fellows over here that hadn't better find them alone." However, we left them alone more than once, and lost nothing, so it is supposable that only the Indians and the "neighbors" found them exposed.

Mr. Purse, who invited us to the festival, besides being President of the Seneca Nation at that time, is a Baptist preacher, a Sunday-School teacher, plays in the brass band, teaches singing school, translates hymns and sets them to music, and sometimes composes both—supervises all the printing done in the language—is the prosecutor of those who sell whiskey to the Senecas, makes speeches to the whites in good English—and is now engaged with some three or four others in translating the New Testament into their tongue. In his wild younger days he travelled over the greater part of North America with a band of musicians, and now seems to be making the best use of all he learned in his peregrinations. Appreciating the advantages of true civilization, as well as the difficulty of bringing them home to his people where they are, and as they are, by any means hitherto used, he has now on foot a new project partly executed, for the more thorough instruction of a part, at least, of the Senecas. He has selected thirty young people of both sexes, whom he desires to get into Christian families in decent neighborhoods, to learn the arts and ways of civilized life, and to get a good school education besides. He has already got places for several, and hopes, by sending out his people to learn, to do what a few teachers among them never could accomplish. He hopes they may be able to maintain themselves by their labor, and thus be no expense either to the whites or themselves. Those already out are doing well.

The white "neighbors" mingled in the festivities, and helped get up the refreshments, and the whole affair went off swimmingly ; but with the exception of dusky faces and the strange language of the dusky speakers, it was like any Sunday-School celebration, animated by a brass band and a feast. True, the gala dresses were somewhat in aboriginal taste, though not in pattern, but it was as civilized as anybody's celebration.

Mr. Purse, whose Indian name I wish I could remember, was, of course, one of the principal orators of the day, and spoke in his grave, earnest, energetic way, that well nigh made his Seneca tongue intelligible to Yankee ears. The closing honors were awarded to our captain, whose speech seemed to please the Indians as much as the Indians had pleased us, one delighted old man asserting in very bad English, that this was " The best speak he ever did heard!" How much of it he understood is problematical. Owing to their appreciation of that speech, however, our friend was invited to preach to them the next day, and had the offer of a canoe to take him to meeting. Of course he went. I rather think he would have done it if he had never done such a thing before, for the poetic inspiration of the place and people seemed to endow him with the spirit to do his best without any trouble.

Before morning, however, there were two considerable dampers cast upon our enthusiasm. The first was the discovery of a complicated sectarian feud existing among them; the nation being divided into the "Old Style" and the "Christian" parties, and the latter being subdivided into the Presbyterian and Baptist parties.

The second damper was a shower in the night, which put our frail wigwam to a test it could not bear. Even the Baptist portion of our party had to put up with being sprinkled that night. It did not rain in the morning, so, as we did not wish to appear to take sides in their feuds, half of us went to the Presbyterian meeting close by the camp, and the other half went down to the picnic ground among the Baptists.

After church we had a taste of the good manners of some stray Ellicottvillians, who were fishing in the river. Some of them were in boats and some on shore, and two of the latter came tearing through our premises, and swung themselves down the bank by the ridge pole of our house, pulling the mansion down after them, just as it began to rain again in good earnest.

We didn't like it, but we couldn't help it, and so we

ran about looking for shelter, like a nest of ants whose home has been unroofed by taking away the flat stone they had encamped under. Back in the woods a piece, just in the edge of a raspberry patch, stood a log cabin covered with boards, unfinished, and never used. There was a hole cut for a door, but no door in it, and a hole in the roof for smoke to go out, but no chimney. The spaces between the logs were unchinked, and there was no flooring. A stray cow seemed to have lodged there occasionally, but we removed all evidence of her former presence, and strewed the floor thickly with hemlock boughs, and having removed ourselves into it, bag and baggage, dried ourselves before a roaring fire built under that hole in the roof. It rained all that night and the next day, and made quite a little freshet, dirtying the clear Allegany sadly, and washing away our springs. The floodwood came down at such a rate that we could not cross the river, and a projected visit to the aged Patriarch Blacksnake, the nephew of the renowned Red Jacket, had to be foregone. That was an irreparable omission, for within the year he died, at the age of one hundred and twenty-three years. The oldest of the nation now living, can remember him as a middle-aged man when they were little children.

As I said before, the gourmands eschewed our company, but for all that, as we were neither spiders, nor snakes, nor angels, we had to eat occasionally, and as our cupboard grew as bare as Mother Hubbard's, we began to think about converting raw materials into eatables— for even savages *cook*, and the utmost simplicity of living we could attain to would not make Allegany mountain trout eatable without fire. I believe I am aboriginal

enough, and hate dishwashing badly enough to make me
satisfied to roast my fish on a stick and eat it from a
leaf, and then throw away my gridiron and plate to save
washing. Thus extremes should meet, for I would at
once be as simple as an anchorite, and as luxurious as
the Emperor of Japan, whose dishes are broken as soon
as used, so that nobody else shall profane them by eating after him, nor he suffer the indignity of eating twice
from the same dish. But my companions thought that
neither the august prestige of the potentate's example,
nor the thriftless laziness of mine, could keep the fish
thus roasted from tasting smoky, nor add the desired
flavor of salt and butter, so there must be so much of
the abjured arts of civilization used as sufficed to fry
fish. Mrs. A. and Susie had provided all sorts of pro-
vender, even down to pots of butter and bags of salt,
but nobody had brought a frying-pan, nor even a "dish
kettle," which one of our ingenious countrywomen has
averred is convertible to every culinary purpose whatever, from a coffee-pot to an oven. Some of our Seneca
neighbors had sent us some peas, and here were peas to
boil and fish to fry, and a pint tin basin and a self-sealing
fruit can, holding a quart, were our utmost resources.
With a stove there would have been little difficulty, but
it rained pitilessly, and our fire was a huge heap of
burning wood on the ground, under that corresponding
huge hole in the roof, which let out all the smoke which
went straight up, and let in all the rain which fell straight
down upon it. The wind, too, took an occasional whim
of introducing variety in the camp, by varying the posi-
tion of the column of smoke and fire from its perpendicular to all sorts of angles between that and the

horizontal, and sometimes whirling it into a spiral shape, which however pretty to look at, took up as inconvenient and uncivil an amount of room, and was something less approachable than a crinoline in a waltz.

Our captain had taken advantage of the morning rain, when trout like to be caught and always bite, and had come home with a fine string of them, and was nothing loth to stand drying his bedraggled length before the log heap; but as he stood looking forlorn enough, a bright idea was working under the touzeled exterior of his caput. He went out and cut a slender beech sapling, some inch and a half through, and stood up gravely again, whittling industriously at his stick. Off fell the leaf-laden branches, hissing and snapping into the fire, as he lopped them away, and finally the sapling seemed a club about eight feet long, split at one end. Into this split, the edge of the pint basin was insinuated, and held by the elastic wood, like Milo's fingers in the log trap he caught himself in, and lo! there was a Lilliputian frying-pan with a Brobdignag handle, and the biggest Professor from our Alma Mater transformed himself into the *chef cuisinier* of our expedition. In went some butter and a coiled up fish, and our extempore skillet was held over the fire by a muscular arm, and watched by a metaphysical eye, as though it was the manliest occupation in the world!

Our captain is a good surveyor, and would make a good engineer they say—is a good mathematician and a good logician—he teaches well and he preaches well—is six feet high—has big whiskers, and a bass voice—and added to all this he improvises frying-pans, and fries fish

capitally. And he looks just as dignified and philosophic
doing that as at anything I ever saw him do. He forbad
our calling him " Professor A——" fifty times, but we
forgot it every time, and he seemed just as professional
in one place and plight as another. He might stand ever
so long *en dishabille* with the water dripping out of his
red flannel shirt, and upon his head from the leaky roof,
and fry trout one at a time for our breakfast, and we
would call him " Professor" in good faith while he was
at it. It was as good as forty lectures on the dignity of
labor. I wondered then, more than ever, where people
ever get the absurd notion of talking about "refined"
and "vulgar," or "masculine and "feminine" employ-
ments. It sounds as ridiculous as the French way of
calling knives masculine and forks feminine. My knives
are no more masculine than my forks. Elvira's shooting
was as feminine as her curls, and the Professor's cooking
as manly as his beard. Susie was as lady-like when she
washed up our scanty dinner service in the frying-pan,
as when she played and sang in her mother's parlor, and
our captain never was more a gentleman in the pulpit
or on the rostrum than when making that frying-pan.
I believe he could darn his own stockings, sew on his
own buttons, or perhaps possibly he might even sell
tape behind a counter, or sit à la Turc on a shopboard
and stitch jackets, and not bate one jot of his manhood.
I exulted as I thought how those brawny hands had carried that massive head up from a poor and obscure place
by their power to work, and thought that so long as the
" mud-sills" of the Bridge of State are made of such
right royal, and at the same time such stubbornly democratic timber as this, the Bridge *cannot* sink—no, not

even under the weight of a "latter-day" President,
Cabinet, and two whole Houses of Congress! But here
I've got clear into both Houses of Congress and our
peas ain't cooked yet! There's velocity for you! I
think I might help Mr. Field and his corps about that
troublesome Atlantic Telegraph! But as my efforts in
that line can hardly be appreciated yet, and as I can
prove a capacity for cooking peas, I will leave that cable
in its sea-salt pickle, and its owners in their monetary
pickle, and tell you how I dulled our poet's jack-knife,
scraping the cement off the old tomato can, in order to
make a dinner pot of it. Somebody says that kind of
cement is poison—the which I don't know—but it is
uncomely and unsavory, so it had to be scraped and
melted and scoured off, and then when the peas were
put in, and the lid on, we had neither bail to hang it by,
nor handle to hold it by, nor stove to set it on. But we
did not mind that, for Necessity, the mother of Inven-
tion, had several of her children with her in our camp.
The Professor could make frying-pans and the Poet could
manufacture shovels. A stray clap-board, gleaned from
a pile of drift-wood by the river, was duly hewn and
whittled into shape and did duty as a shovel, and was,
from a respectful distance, thrust into our little volcano,
and robbing it of a pile of coals, our extempore dinner
pot was set thereon, and cooked away with profound
satisfaction.

The Europeans laugh at the American propensity for
whittling, and no doubt it is ridiculous sometimes, but
it is a natural consequence of plenty of wood and few
tools, and our experience proved jack-knives to be a
great institution.

We would ask you to dinner if you would not be scandalized at the scantiness of our dinner service. One table-knife and fork, three jack-knives and a pen-knife, two spoons and two plates, and, it must be confessed, our *dinner-pot* and *frying-pan* added to our two tin drinking cups, was the whole. It would have been better for each to have carried a private spoon in a side-pocket, but we didn't think of it, and so we waited for each other when we had " spoon victuals," and at other times did what our ancestors did before forks were invented—used five-pronged implements like those Mother Eve managed with native grace in the bowers of Paradise.

Nobody can tell till he has tried it, how much fun there is in doing without things. It is really astonishing how many things people can do without, when they can't help it. Altogether the merriest meals I ever helped to eat, were thus merry not on account of what we *had*, but on account of what we had *not*. Some absurd and irremediable omission provokes mirth, where people are not silly enough to feel chagrined at the poverty or the blunder. If we had made our outfit perfect, and had forgotten nothing, we should not have had so many things to laugh at, and should probably have enjoyed it less.

Next day the heavens " stopped crying," and we went up the river in a wagon, and slept in a house on a floor that night. The air seemed very close after the airy chambers we had been occupying.

There is a "Rock City " on a ridge of hill near Great Valley, where conglomerate rocks are piled many feet high for several miles in length. Here in a

crevice of the rocks part of our company encamped
the ensuing night. Feathery ferns and mosses tufted
the rocks and trees, but the shade was too deep for any
luxuriance of undergrowth. Some of us got a bit of a
ducking in crossing Great Valley Creek to get there.
The bridge was gone, and the water so deep that it
floated our wagon-box and wetted our bedding. It got
dried, however, and none of us got drowned.

Here my western enemy, the ague, which had tormented me through Illinois " and back again," like the
champion in the old game, who couldn't succeed in
dodging the old witch on the way to Bileybright, came
on with double force and drove me home. When I lay
sick and fevered by the Mississippi, drinking. warm
wiggling water, I felt as though the cool springs and
clear air of these hills would cure me at once—but it
took more than one week.

On my way to the dépôt I visited one more curiosity, and one yet unexplained. This was the " breathing well." It looks at the top like any ordinary well
dug for domestic purposes in a farm-house door-yard,
and this was its original design, but after digging some
thirty feet they came to a strong current of air, but no
water. They dug no further, but put a sort of pen-
stock in the top of the well, with a large tin whistle
fitted into it, which answers every purpose of a barome-
ter. When the air is light the current rushes out of the
well with great force, blowing away anything which is
laid over the hole, and blowing the whistle like a young
steam engine. If the air without is heavy, the well
draws in its breath with the same energy.

The cause of this phenomenon is unknown, being

theoretically supposed to be owing to some hypothetical cavern down there somewhere. It is worth the investigation of the curious.

My companions pursued their way to visit the new coal-mines a few miles south of here in Pennsylvania, but as a true historian's tale must stop where his knowledge does, I must pause here. If you are as sorry as I was, I am glad.

I once heard an enthusiastic Geologist say, that when he was a confirmed and almost hopeless invalid, he took daily doses of the Tertiary Formation for one season, and found himself well. He had been a close student, and had contracted an inveterate dyspepsia, which, he was told, exercise would cure. His first attempt was a signal failure. Every day he started for a walk, in the spirit of swallowing a dose of pills, and walked along absorbed in his books, or else thinking about his ailments, saying to himself continually, "This is to cure the dyspepsia; this rod is to leave the dyspepsia one more rod behind; so much exercise vs. so much dyspepsia," &c. &c. But he found after a six weeks' trial, that giving his distresses an airing only increased them, and the more he tired himself, trying to walk off his indigestion, the more it would not be walked off.

A Naturalist spent a few days with him, and his thoughts became keenly interested in the earth-history recorded beneath his feet. With the whole energy of his excitable temperament he threw himself into the study of Geology, and in pursuing the thread of its revelations among the hills and along watercourses, down wells, and up precipices, his aches and ails vanished.

The keen out-of-door interest he had gained, carried out his thoughts from the sphere of their chronic habits, and with every breath of air that filled his lungs, the

now bounding pulses poured the once creeping blood
into their vitalizing laboratory.

The pulsations of the aroused soul stirred the half
stagnant currents of the body, and renewed their life in
the free air. His disease was lost off and forgotten.
He no longer thought of inspecting his tongue at the looking glass, nor feeling his pulse, nor keeping an account
of the variations of his appetite. He had something far
more interesting to think of, and the added relish it
gave to the minutiæ of life was enjoyed without analysis or reflection. He did not ask of himself how much
such or such an organ had been benefited, in order to
enable it to afford him such and such a pleasure more
than usual. He had always led some such forced and
methodical existence before, but now he led a spontane-
ous life, and the long dormant seeds of many joys began
to swell and sprout within him. He was no longer the
pasteboard globe revolving on pivots within its wooden
horizon and brazen meridian, but a planet rolling through
space, with infinite blue on every hand, and the kindly
influence of many moons and stars drawing him in an
eccentric and wavering orbit around his central sun.

How could he remember to have the dyspepsia then?

Half the diseases of mankind would get well of themselves if they were not so petted and thought about.
Many a common cold has been worried into consumption and the grave, by constant attention and apprehen-
sion. We are perpetually warned against being careless
or negligent of our physical disorders, and the warning
is sometimes needed; but it as often happens that the
continual reminding us of it aggravates the difficulty, as
it happens that care alleviates it.

3

We generally find what we look for in this world, and
in this field as truly as anywhere. If we look into every
coughing fit for the seeds of bronchitis or consumption,
we will find them after a while, and if we watch them
incessantly to see them germinate, by and by sure
enough, they will begin to grow, when, if we had not
used our anxiety and attention as a sort of hot-house .
and forcing-bed for them, they never would have vege-
tated. I have known a spinal disease to be induced by
constantly thinking about and expecting it, and daily
looking over one's shoulders into a glass to detect a cur-
vature. People go mad, sometimes, for fear they will
be crazy.

They say that Pan, the genius of the woods, is dead,
and that his mistress, Nature, went out of fashion long
ago, and is quite obsolete in polite circles now; yet if
there is a *pathy* in the world, worthy of trust, it is that
taught in their school.

Hydropathy, as practised by Naiades and Undines,
must be delightful in warm weather, but the difficulty
of finding the physicians at home when you call, makes
its efficacy uncertain. But Pan, who may have died,
and come to life again, for aught I know, is alive now,
and always at home. Kill him ever so many times, he
won't stay dead. He has more lives than a cat, and
what is better, he has the power of transferring his
vital tenacity to his patients. He is the greatest of
physicians, although mythology says nothing about it,
and though his bill is not the longest. He has other
modes of advertising the superiority of their mode of
cure, than making magnificent charges. There is no
quackery about the Nature Cure. It never orders nau-

scous poisons to be forced into the stomach, in the expectation that they will find some road to the liver or pancreas, or other ungetatable places, when they are out of order. To be sure, other doctors do it, but that does not hinder the venomous medicine from finding the wrong road just as easily as the right one, and blundering into the wrong gland, or some other place, and go to curing what is not sick, just as fast as what is.

This is a different system. The man who took the tertiary strata did not swallow them, though he took them in ether—a sort of ether that keeps best without bottling up or corking. Yet it was an internal application, acting with great force on the brain and all the vital organs, although so agreeable to take, that it soon became more delightful than any feast, the only disagreeable results being the fatigue consequent upon so much exercise. But what sweet sleep followed those days of toil, and what pleasant dreams grew out of the invigorating atmosphere he breathed all day long!

An invalid who does not feel quite equal to the task of carrying a stone hammer and a basket of rocks over the hills, as a sanitary measure, can of course take a different prescription. For instance, I have known a professional man, addicted to liver complaint and other bad habits, take half an acre of cabbages with excellent effect.

Another, who ought to have sued his ancestors for damages for imposing on him a poor, rickety constitution, contrived to renovate and make it quite passably useful, by the application of five-and-twenty varieties of rose-bushes, with pinks and geraniums *ad libitum*.

That this mode of cure is always accessible, at least

to all country people, is one of its chief recommendations. Skilled physicians of any other school are so
often uugetatable, that the children of poverty must
submit to be experimented upon by tyros and quacks,
or go unattended through sickness, unless they have
faith to try the out-of-door treatment, which, in a great
majority of cases, if taken soon enough, will perform a
cure ; and if it fails, and the patient dies, he has at least
the satisfaction of dying a natural death, without the
assistance of the Faculty.

There is much truth in the old proverb, " An ounce
of prevention is worth a pound of cure." All physicians of every school will say, that any disease is much
easier cured, if taken in time, than if deferred as long
as possible. Some diseases of the most formidable character—contagious, hideous, and often fatal—may be
wholly averted, if proper steps be taken before exposure
to infection; and greatly modified after it, so as to be
neither frightful nor dangerous, if properly treated from
the moment of their inception—as for instance the
small-pox. Let it alone, and it will kill or disfigure its
victim. Vaccinate or diet, and he will come out whole
and sound in most cases. We claim no miraculous
power of restoration is to be found, even in the purest
air of the mountain-tops; but a vigorous preventive,
and a salutary, healing influence for those inclined to
disease, or already partially ailing, is plentiful and free.
Mother Nature herself would not take a far-gone consumptive into her hospital. When a man gets too ill
to get out of doors, it is too late for him to try that
method of cure, and often too late for any method to
do him any good. If you had a friend going to be

hanged, you would not wait until the rope was about his neck, before you started to get him reprieved ; but when our friends sicken, we think it is time enough to do something when they can no longer sit up or eat their meals. The wonder is, not that people so often die young, but that anybody lives to be old. It exhibits an almost incredible tenacity of life, for a sedentary person to get well after a fit of illness.

Divers spasmodic efforts to restore the regime of Nature in the medical world, have risen and waned, alternately astonishing the world by their audacity, and amusing it by their absurdities. But the passion for humbug and mock erudition which has always more or less characterized this profession, and the fact that it is and has been a *profession* instead of a study, a science, and an art, have made these new schools ruin themselves by their Brobdignag pretensions and Lilliputian achievements. The little fire of truth under this witches' cauldron of medicaments and theories, has kept the uncanny broth bubbling, and these ephemeral attempts at reform have been but the bursting bubbles on its surface.

. A European school of Empirics once professed to have discovered that the breath of cattle was the most curative atmosphere an invalid could inhale, and prescribed in certain chronic diseases that the patient should be laid on a pallet in front of the feeding racks of the cattle, in order to breathe in, and otherwise absorb, the hygienic odors of the kine.

People have been sent to the tops of mountains to regain the health they might have kept if they had only visited the mountain tops on their own feet sooner, instead of waiting to use the feet of mules, when their own were no longer available.

They have been sent to the bottom of caverns for the nitrous air, that was to heal the lungs that were decaying because they had never had enough of any sort of air. Pale students and professional men who have made their offices the ante-rooms to the Court of Death, by breathing dust and carbonic acid, and the fumes of ink and tobacco, from one year's end to the other, run under ground in Mammoth cave to escape yet a little longer the final putting under ground, which they have not dreaded enough to avoid sooner.

Merchants, from whose abused nostrils the everlasting smells of the shop and store seldom have a chance to subside, take costly pilgrimages to far off springs, to drink abominable waters, to undo the evil that never would have befallen them if they had breathed more clean air, and drunk more pure water, as they went along.

Ladies who have squeezed the breath of life out of their lungs, and admitted the chills of death to their bare arms and shoulders, and might-as-well-be bare feet, go into the sea brine with the lobsters, after the health that grows thriftily in the kitchen garden and on every hillside.

Thrifty housewives who fry their vital juices out over the cooking stove, and fill their lungs with evaporated dinners, and their stomachs with indigestible delicacies, generally take to patent medicines and kindred abominations to purge them of their unnecessary ailments. They, seldomer than any other class, think they can afford time, or have strength to take any part in the Nature cure the others try to get at.

·I sometimes think women like to be sick, they take such capital care to destroy any health they may have inherited. They think frail health is interesting. Don't the poets write delightfully maudlin verses about beautiful consumptives coughing away their forlorn existence in the most sentimental manner possible? Romantic young ladies, with rosy cheeks and bright eyes, feel complimented at having some simpleton insinuate that theirs is the radiant eye and hectic flush of incipient phthisis. Health is vulgar. No fashionable lady will own to so prosaic a condition. Did you ever hear one say right heartily, without any modification of *ifs* or *buts*, that she was in excellent health? Not she! If nothing under the sun ails her, she will sooner improvise a pain in her side, or her head, or her little finger, or her great toe, rather than be supposed to have no ailment whatever. She thinks it prettier to be sick; and for fear she might be well if she let herself alone, she exposes her extremities to the vicissitudes of the atmosphere, and crushes in her vitals with jean and whalebones, and loads the lower viscera and vertebræ with a young camel's load of dry goods and hardware to drag down her life and impede locomotion. Of course no animal thus loaded, hoppled, cramped, and exposed, can apply the nature cure without altering her habits and defying fashion, and this few women are brave enough to do. She prides herself on being a coward (" timid " is the euphemistic phrase), for that is almost as necessary as ill health to make a lady interesting. " She might as well be out of the world, as out of fashion," and so she puts herself out of the world as expeditiously as the prevailing mode of suicide prescribes. No matter for the Divine command, "Thou shalt not kill!" Fashion says, "Kill yourselves and your children by slow torture!" and Goddess Fashion is obeyed, and the Lord's commandment broken. *Murder* is a stern word with which to confront and accuse these delicate dames, but what less have they done? If they like not my speech, I commend them to the third chapter of the poems of the Prophet Isaiah, and pass on.

Young ladies in their teens, who have resolution enough to defy parental advice and authority, and run away with some perfumed popinjay, to be "married in haste to repent at leisure," have not moral force nor physical courage enough to put on a pair of calfskin shoes, and a dress short and loose enough to climb hills in without stepping on the skirts, or gasping for the breath they have no room for in their dress waists; and then, thus equipped, to take rambles, and even scrambles, in places rough and smooth in pursuit of those objects of beauty or curiosity, of scientific or artistic interest, which are always accessible in the woods and fields.

No, indeed! *Scientific young ladies are never the heroines of novels!* They are absurd and unfashionable, and are supposed always to have ragged blue stockings, inky fingers, and dowdy hair. They are believed to be predestined to be old maids, or the worthless wives of victimized husbands, and the slatternly mothers of neglected children. All the oracles of romance have shown that women never take to science or art, except from starvation or disappointment.

I am not going to dispute her prey with Romance, for her votaries are too destitute of gumption to be brought to their senses by anything short of the sharpest realities of life, and then it is often too late for them to undo the absurd mischiefs they have done to themselves.

Romance makes the confectionery of life, but whoever undertakes to live on sweetmeats must pay the penalty of such folly.

Half the American people are women, or will be, if they live long enough, but how is the nation to stand alone with so flimsy a " better half" as these women make ? The mass of American women work as hard or harder than the men, but they accomplish far less, because they work at an immense disadvantage. Even the women of the country do themselves up in such a way that if they were perfect Sampsons they could not do much but tire themselves out in trying to do. Put Sampson himself in hoops and long skirts, and set him to carrying up full pans of milk from the cellar dairy room, and see how he would make out. Set him to hoeing the kitchen garden, or weeding onion beds, and after he had tripped himself up a few times by treading on his " flowing, graceful drapery," and after thereby ripping it loose from the waist, and tearing and muddying it in sundry places, see if he wouldn't swear, or "think swear " at least. If he had had on a long-shouldered dress, and shoulder braces, when he met the lion, I'm thinking the bees might have found another hive than the lion's body, unless the lion had worn corsets too, in which case the man might have killed him.

Suppose you send him out in a lady's rig to do an errand, in a high wind, and see how, with all sails set, he could make headway against the storm. Let him feel all sorts of things flapping, scourging, entangling, twisting, jerking, snapping, and dragging away at every part of him, and he would cry out, like Cain, that his punishment was greater than he could bear. Call woman the "weaker vessel" indeed! If she were not stronger than Sampson, and more patient than Job, she *could* not, and *would* not submit to the fatigues and inconveniences of such habits, and if she were not sillier than a goose she would not be the slave of raiment that she is.

But what with fashions, and fashion-plate magazine literature, and customs and prejudice, it will be hard work to induce young women, who are the very class who need it most, to take that out-door exercise that their health and highest intelligence demands.

The assertion that the highest intelligence needs exercise of the body in fresh air, in order for its development, may be disputed. Those whose idea of intellectuality are all connected with pallor and leanness will cite all manners of cripples and invalids, to show how energetically the mind may work in a disordered body. I know that Scott and Byron were lame, but I know, too, that they walked and swam as few sound men do. I know that Elizabeth Browning is feeble, and that she wrote better when she was well, and that her sea-side rambles have left their impress on her poetry. Charlotte Bronte inherited a consumption, and was "stunted" by starvation in childhood, but if she had not habitually taken longer walks over the bleak Yorkshire moors than an American lady would think possible, we should never have had Jane Eyre, nor heard of its author. Harriet Martineau, though incurably diseased and deaf, has written the best guide-book for the wild and rugged lake scenery amid which she lives that has ever been written. Because, not only was she more gifted than other guide-book authors, but she was practically more familiar with what she describes.

These are the sick ones, but the well ones are in the majority. Most sickly geniuses die before they arrive at such celebrity, or indeed before they get out of their teens. Think of Bayard Taylor or Ida Pffeifer hobbling round the world on crutches, or scaring the sea nymphs of Pacific or Indian seas, with the ghostly pallor of their dyspeptic visages, or the hectic gleam of sunken eyes! Imagine Banvard, or Church, or Rosa Bonheur painting the Father of Waters, the Heart of the Andes, or the Horse Fair from luxurious carriages, in embroidered slippers and kid gloves! If Hiram Powers had remained an indoor man in a Cincinnati warehouse, or Harriet Hosmer a parlor ornament or kitchen utensil in her Massachusetts home, do you think that we should have ever had the Greek Slave or Zenobia?

It took a sea-side cave for a study, and an audience of waves, to train a Demosthenes of old, and a hunter's life among Virginia's hills to make a Patrick Henry of modern times. The life of the wandering " flower-girl of the Boulevards " ripened into Rachel, the Queen of Tragedy; and how much had the wild air of the Polar region to do in developing the gifts of that Swedish song-bird, Jenny Lind?

It takes a well oxygenized blood to stimulate the brain to healthy action. Carbonic acid mixed with the purple currents of life, does not agree with the nucleus of the nervous system. Genius itself must succumb to half-vitalized blood and a vitiated atmosphere. The " midnight lamp " addles more brains than it enlightens. There is philosophy in the old notion that moonlight

crazes people, that is, if they stay awake of nights to
look at it. Nature forbids over activity as well as sloth,
and haunting about at uncanny hours, as well as staying
shut up at all hours.

These two absurd notions, that it is not pretty to be
robust and rosy, and that it is pretty to try to superin-
duce beauty or genius by making owls of ourselves in
turning night into day, or by rat-like inhabiting unven-
tilated and unwholesome quarters, seem, in stating, too
ridiculous and foolish to require a rebuff or refutation;
and yet there are multitudes of our fellow-creatures and
creaturesses acting upon them daily. ·

Why else do our ruddy, stalwart farmer boys seek
to be doctors and clerks, as though goods and drugs
smelled sweeter than fresh mould or clover sod? They
think white hands measuring tape and assorting fancy
buttons, or fingering deranged pulses, are much more
stylish and "genteel," than honest sunbrowned hands.
They think a varnished and useless cane a more interesting and elegant occupant of their digits than rake or
plough handles would be. And why else do fat and rosy
young ladies drink vinegar and eat chalk and tea-
grounds to diminish their flesh and color, if they do
not think health and strength undesirable? Or why
do would-be geniuses keep late hours, and roll their
eyes ominously, if they do not receive these notions?

We may ignore this large and increasing class of
dunces, and treat only of those we generally think of as
the more sensible class, who are the vigorous doers of
the land, and yet we shall not find them obeying the
laws of life any better than the others. They may
plead the excuse that they are wearing out for some

purpose, and not from sheer folly; but I know not that the Divine command, "Thou shalt not kill!" makes any exceptions in favor of those who work themselves to death.

Mankind seem not to have learned that however much the body may bear of abuse, it is the worse for every ill thing done to it. A man may be sick and get well again, yet that illness has shortened his life. He expends his health recklessly, and says that he is strong, and can bear the strain of his unnatural living; but though the machinery may endure " by reason of strength even to fourscore years," the fresh vigor of life that might have been retained, has gone long before that, and a man of seventy now, is older than Adam was at six hundred.

Even wise men say that the times demand a rapidity of action which cannot be sustained except by unnatural stimulus and expenditure of vital energy. The spirit of the times demands that we should hurry ourselves to death, eating, drinking, sleeping, and working, with a deadly activity, which prevents any of these things being done thoroughly.

Why this scrambling haste? Have you not time to live *well* while you are about it? We Americans are in such a desperate hurry we have not time even to chew our dinners before they are swallowed. We can't wait for the cars to stop before we jump upon the platform, nor wait for the steamboat to be moored before we leap across a nice place in which to drown, in order to get on board or on shore. We count it wasted time to do slowly what it is possible to do rapidly even to live. The deliberate philosophy has few votaries among our countrymen. Because man is not a ruminating animal, he seems to think he needs no time for chewing anything but gum or tobacco, and these he chews as he runs.

To move leisurely along the ways of existence, in order to let the experiences of life have full time to mature their proper fruit in the character, is considered too slow for the Age; and so this double high pressure engine Age drives everybody as if life were a general racecourse, where he who gets through quickest wins the stakes. Few of us like even slow, solemn, and grand music; a waltz or quickstep better pleases us.

All our inventions are for hurrying up the processes known before, or contriving more rapid ones to supersede them; and we partake of the character of our inventions. We cannot wait even for hides to be tanned into leather by the tedious processes of the old time, but rot them by more rapid and less substantial and efficacious methods. It is the same with most of our fabrics. Dispatch, rather than durability and excellence, is the prevailing idea in the manufacture of everything from college Baccalaureates to shoe pegs.

We have thus created a false and flimsy taste among us, which, from having few substantial things which would endure the wear and tear of time, has made us come to like the incessant change; and if we do happen to have anything last beyond the ephemeral existence of its contemporaries, we get tired of it, and demolish it on purpose. People get tired of durable garments,— have had them so long they are sick of them. They get out of conceit of beautiful houses which have outlasted the style in vogue when they were built, and pull down the excellent old house only because it is out of fashion, and build another not as good but more fashionable, in its place.

Even old men and women are out of fashion, and if there is now and then one, they are the odd exceptions and not the rule. The unavoidable evil, when it does come, is concealed as far as possible by all manner of arts and affectations, as though old age were no longer honorable.

Thus we have destroyed our faculty of veneration by destroying what is venerable among us. As we measure age, our nation itself will soon be old and in its dotage, and must make way for some newer style of government, or some old style come round new again, as our styles of dress are renewed.

This absurd and destructive racing system must either rush us into this and other undesirable results and catastrophes, or be abated and cooled off, and taught to go slower. So long as we are proud of our rapidity there is little hope of mending it. We must meet some overwhelming disaster or disgrace, to humiliate us, if we will learn wisdom from nothing but experience. If nothing but rushing into the gap of an open drawbridge will· convince our fast engineers that the car of state has no wings, why we must have a general crash, as on our railroads.

But those of us who love smooth waters and quiet scenes, can at least set before our fast countrymen and women the dangers of haste, and the open and inviting fields of health and recreation, where the overtasked and broken down may regain in fresh and quiet pursuits, that strength they have destroyed by their over hasty living.

It is pitiful to see the pale and hollow cheeks, and the languid and drooping figures, of so many of our young men and women whose vital energies were originally sufficient to have carried them bravely on to a green old age, if they had not been used up by false living, and so left them old and worn out in their prime. There is no artificial process of renovation. The decayed teeth may be replaced, but the torture of the process will leave its pain brand on the face, like a wrinkle of age. The grey hair may be dyed, but the white roots will be continually showing at the parting. The body's bones may be hidden by drapery and wadding, but the sallow skin hanging loose upon the skeleton of the hands and neck, betrays the waste of life within. The skin may be daubed with whiting and paint, only to be a mockery without, and a slowly absorbed and deadly poison within. A full beard may hide a sunken cheek, but not a sunken eye. Cloves and cardamom seeds, and orris root or perfumery, may conceal a pestilent breath, but not the cough that belongs to it. Poetry may decorate disease, but can never make it pleasant or beautiful.

If one can be well, it is morally wrong to be sick. We deserve better of ourselves than to murder our good bodies that the dear Lord gave us to take care of our souls with. If we do it carelessly and ignorantly, still the penalty falls upon us. There is a death-penalty attached to these physical transgressions, and whoso breaks the laws of life is a self-murderer.

There are things worth dying for, but how many of us who transgress the life laws do it in a cause worth the cost?

You whose flying feet crush the life out of so many

trooping moments as they come, and whirl yourselves
dizzily through stifling rooms into the cold air, that cuts
its way through your heated lungs, to the very seat of
life—you who have giddily danced the "Dance of Death,"
was your pleasure worth the life ye forfeited for it?

And you, dismal Ascetics, who believe that God only
loves long faces, and who evólve ponderous sermons out
of your bile and dyspepsia, darkening the beautiful
sunshine and the joyous smiles of life with your raven
shadow, and drowning its gushing laughter and song
with your croaking and groans,—when the acrid acidity
of your lives corrodes your health away, and brings
you down to death,—do you think that your gall and
vinegar temper, which you mistook for piety, was worth
the life it cost?

Servants of Fashion! Has your capricious mistress
ever repaid you for the corns she has pinched on your
toes, the breath she has crushed from your lungs, the
curves she has given your spines, the perpetual incon-
venience and expense she has cost you, and above all
for the wasted hours and shortened life she has caused?

Slaves of Luxury and Appetite! Where are the
rewards of your fearful sacrifices? The ancients cast
their infants into the fiery embrace of their brazen
Moloch as an offering, but you have consumed yourselves by slow tortures as living, yet dying, sacrifices to
your terrible Idols! Item by item have your bodies
been diseased and tortured to pay the penalty of your
devotion to Appetite. Gout and dyspepsia, tooth-ache
and liver-complaint, cholera and delirium tremens, apo-
plexy and heart disease, nervous torment and lunacy,
are the rewards of your indulgence in the pleasures of

Appetite, Luxury, and Indolence; and the loss of life, the extreme penalty the body can pay, is the end of it in this world. You have eaten and drunken and revelled, at the price of your lives. Were your debauches worth their cost?

Devotees of wealth, what reward have ye? Lives of toil and bondage, to gather, *what?* You have denied yourselves the free gifts of air and exercise perhaps, or have worked beyond your strength, and have accumulated *dust* for those who outlive you to quarrel about! You have deferred life until rich enough to live, and now you die. Have you not sold life too cheaply?

Ambition's votaries, who have wrought with all your force to make a niche in the temple of Fame, where you might dwell and be admired of mankind, what reward have ye? Disappointment and envy and death! Are you paid for your lives?

Oh! all ye whose lives have been a feverish strife after some imaginary good, come and slake your thirst and cool your fever in the clear waters of the many springs among the hills. Let nature's breath breathe into your failing lungs the healing of her own. Let the serenity of Nature steal upon your unrest, and give you her tranquillity. Allow the vigor of her unfailing forces to renew your lives. Let the great pulses of her ever beating heart throb with your own.

Thus even hereditary taints of disease in the constitution may be overcome in a measure, and the burden of pain earned by those who come before us, and not by ourselves, may be removed.

I should find it hard to pardon my ancestors for my existence in the flesh, if what they had given me were leprous, or scrofulous, or consumptive, or predisposed to insanity or special vice. Yet I see many of my fellow creatures have existence thrust upon them thus burdened and cursed. We see distorted, deformed, diseased, and crippled wretches, who are so from no choice of their own, but because they were the infant sacrifices devoted to the Moloch of their parents' appetites and passions, or their cruelties and mistakes.

These unfortunates seldom have the mental or moral vigor sufficient to reverse the process of destruction begun by their progenitors, and by living in accordance with the natural laws, rescue themselves from a progressive march from torment to torment in the abused flesh. Too commonly they go on as their fathers did, and increase instead of arresting the inherited plague. The son of the drunkard, who has inherited the hideous disease of his father, feeds this morbid appetite with the poison which adds to its craving, and he is sooner a drunkard, and more incurable, than his parent. The child of gross and vicious parents inherits not only the physical consequences of their transgression, but a passional bias in the same direction with the parents, and will be liable to re-enact their deeds, and so suffer an aggravated and double penalty. But those whose mental perceptions and moral force are sufficient to turn them to the simple and efficacious regimen prescribed by Natural Law, will be likely to find healing and health in it.

For the remaining few invalids, not included in the foregoing, who are ill by accident, and not in consequence of the culpable ignorance or wickedness of any body, there is as much hope in the Nature cure as in any. Not that Nature will set broken bones or dislocated joints, but she will have very much to do with curing when they are set.

I wish not to undervalue any profession, but to give nature her due, and she is above all physicians. Moreover, the claims of the suffering are paramount to the claims of all the professions under the sun. Doctors, as such, have no claims on the public, except as they heal the sick better than they would be healed without them.

The plea that we should patronize the various hotels, shops, schools, artizans, members of the professions, etc., in order to *sustain them*, seems to me to be arrant twaddle. What claim have they to sustenance? They are for certain uses, and in so far as they are of use, use them, but no further. If they are not sufficiently useful to command support by their benefits, let them fall. Any institution, or in general any individual who cannot stand alone, with at most a little propping to begin with, might better fall than pretend to stand. Who props up the seedling pine in the forest to make it grow straight, and not fall down from weakness? If one cannot grow from the centre outward, self-balanced, and fast by his own roots, and be helped to grow only for the indispensable fruit he bears, he had better relinquish his ambition to be a tree, and be only what his own power and capacities would make him. Let your supernumerary doctors and lawyers, etc., take to ditching or ploughing, or some of the trades that are never full, and in which it is hardly possible to have a superfluity. If there were no other way to prevent doctors from starving, except to use their services when we didn't want them, there might be some charity in patronizing them, especially if that were cheaper than paying a pauper tax to support them in another, but analogous way. But as circumstances are, where is the need? Let us appeal to the Great Physician out of doors, and let the M.D.'s do as they like, if they do not interfere with us. Surely they have no right to feel aggrieved if we only let them alone. It is often the very best thing we can do by anybody, to let them be. We will give them full opportunity to mind their own business, by minding ours. If we need them we will ask for them, and such patronage will not be a charity nor a humiliation to the man who feels he does only what is needed, and is paid only for what he has done. Good physicians agree that they are only nature's aids; and bad ones, who set up in opposition to her, are those we wish to see driven into some less destructive employment.

Come then into the fields and watch the bright-eyed toads catch flies, and learn of them how to trill the French R; or go down by the marshes and look for "Pete," whom you hear so many little frogs calling for. Perhaps he is the very doctor who can cure you. Or go into the woods and look for bright spotted lizards under the stones and old chunks of rotten wood, or watch the woodpecker listening like the veriest eavesdropper, at all the cracks of the dead tree, to hear what the grubs are saying, ere he opens the door with his bill, and arrests the incipient beetle at his dinner. Go into the beech woods and watch the squirrel stuff his cheeks with the triangular nuts, and go frisking off to his hole, without seeming in the least encumbered by his loaded pouches. See the pigeons scratch up the dead leaves like so many of the most beautiful and graceful of hens, laying bare the sprouting beechnuts they wish to carry to their young; or if you are able, follow them to their nesting place, and see acres and miles of these beautiful creatures at home among their fat squabby babies, and try to estimate the amount of life stirring the air there, and you will begin to feel as if you were absorbing the superabundant and overflowing vitality into your own systems.

" Go to grass." It will do you good; if it does not, it is an error easily repented of, and a course easily abandoned, and one that will leave no poison in the system nor sting in the conscience. But try it, and rest assured, on the experience of those who have tried the experiment, that greens will be good for you, if properly taken.

I hope yet to see invalids giving their full faith only to that school of medicine whose basis of operations is as broad as all-out-of-doors.

THE NATURE CURE.—FOR THE MIND.

PEOPLE, especially the young, often get a diseased appetite for excitement and artificial amusements, and what is called society, to the exclusion of far better things; not because the taste was originally depraved, but because life has presented to them no real and abiding interest.

It is common to hear such persons declare in hours of reaction and discontent, that they find nothing worth living for; they find no pursuit worth all the toil and trouble it costs, and no aim worthy of life. The pleasures they devour last but a little while, and continual change and new excitements are craved with perpetual hunger, which no amount of feeding ever satisfies—the only satiety being spiritual dyspepsia and disgust.

Men usually seek refuge in business from the hungry needs of their inner selves, and try to quench their soul's perennial thirst with eager draughts of gain. Like Midas, they seek to turn all that they touch into gold; and when it is done, they find themselves like him, starving at their own banquets, because gold is neither food nor drink.

Women commonly seek their refuge in matrimony, only to find themselves called upon to feed instead of being fed; and behold their garners are empty and their fountains dry—they perish of thirst and starvation of mind and heart, and others perish with them; so we see the world peopled with the famished skeletons of men and women, who seem, Prometheus-like, to be for ever renewed, but to be for ever devoured by the craving vultures of immortal want and undying need.

To convince us that this condition is abnormal and unnatural, we need only look at nature's ever fresh tranquillity.

To cure it in its chronic state, is only possible to Infinite Grace—a physician not often applied to for that purpose.

Wisdom will avert the disease in the beginning, or find it easily cured in its earlier stages, the chief difficulty being to get other people to allow the patient to take the prescription, not because it is difficult or dangerous, but because the few who admit the existence of the disease despise the simplicity of the remedy. If it were some great thing, they would believe in it, but what is the use of leaving the big Pharpar and Abana to go and wash in that little Jordan?

But the mass deny the existence of the disease, and the necessity of cure, just as madmen rave that they are not mad.

Others say that this is a want for which there is no supply, a disease for which there is no cure. Man was born to hunger and thirst unfed—to suffer unrelieved. This life must be barren and starved, that in the life to come we may have more abundance. It is a doom from which there is no appeal—a fate from which there is no escape.

They might as well say that children were made on purpose to cry, and that their mothers ought to starve them in the cradle, to make them "laugh and grow fat" when they are men.

It seems to be a sort of general belief that people ought to be treated by the rule of contrary, and supplied with exactly the things they do not want. When a *body* is naked they give it sermons, and when it is hungry, spiritual advice; but when the *soul* is starving scholars feed it with Latin and Metaphysics, common folks offer it pork and potatoes, or perhaps a new coat or bonnet, and too often religionists only give it creeds and formulas and beliefs, instead of the bread and water of life; and when the *mind* is hungry they give it no meat, when athirst they give it no drink, when sick and in prison they minister not unto it, because they cannot comprehend the perishing need.

To know, is as positive and keen a want of the mind as hunger is of the body, or grace of the guilty soul.

As everybody recognises the necessity of food for the body, and in this country most people believe in the need of aliment for the moral part of the human trinity, I pass to that part of our hungering which the great mass of the people think may go unfed.

They can see no use in so much learning. What will be done with it? If one can read, and write, and cypher, he has enough to do business, and be " respectable," and what more would he have? There are not wanting those in our midst who think it a waste of time and money to buy and read books; and some of our next-door neighbors think that knowledge tends to knavery and pride, and eschew it accordingly. Said one of this class to a poor school-teacher, " Why in the world do you keep pinching yourself, and working and saving, just to send yourself to school? You know enough to teach school now, you ought to be satisfied

4

and *be like other folks.*". "But what shall I *do*, if I do
not go to school?" asked the girl. "Oh! dress yourself up and *catch a man*, and get married and settle
down, and have a home of your own." "And what
then?" was the query, not asked often enough, by the
way, but the answer was only that she was to do then
as others did. A daughter of one of this sort of
people importuned for the privilege of mental improvement, but was stopped with the information that
" she knew enough to keep house," and that "the
*boys wouldn't like her any better if she knew ever so
much.*" "She *could not make better johnny-cakes* if
she should go to school or study ever so much "—
which must have been immensely consoling to a hungry
mind.

One of our neighbors, a rich farmer, had a son who
worked faithfully for his father until he was twenty
years old, with only a scanty chance of going occasionally to the district school. At last the youth, with a
keen sense of his own deficiencies in learning, besought
his parent to allow him to go *one term* to a sort of an
Academy some twenty miles distant. Consent was
grudgingly wrung by hard teazing, from the father, and
a very spare wardrobe and *a single shilling* furnished
the young man with all the outfit and means his generous parent thought worth while to "throw away" on
"book learning." And this was not in Tartary nor
"Borio-boola Gha," nor in the dark ages, but in the
United States, in the middle of the nineteenth century.
This kind of mental starvation is terribly common too,
though these people would feel grievously slandered if
accused of starving their families; but what better have

they done? Unfortunately, too many of these hungry minds get used to being starved after a while; and though they do not quite die, they pine and wither away, until what might have been vigorous and majestic intellects are stunted dwarfs, nourished with meagerest scraps of food, and watered with vain regrets.

Set before the mass of people, any form of knowledge not absolutely necessary to use in the getting of food and shelter, and they ask, "Of what use is it?" This question must be answered according to their own ideas of use, if they are answered at all. It may be as well worth while to answer the ignorant according to his ignorance, as to "answer a fool according to his folly," as scripture recommends. You can put on a wise look, and give them what will be an answer to them. Tell them that geology will teach men how to find coal and lime, and metals; that botany will teach what plants are poisonous, and what are eatable, and what are good for medicine; that entomology will teach where to look for cutworms, how to get rid of caterpillars, and how' to manage bees; astronomy will tell when the moon changes and when the tide will be high, and will help men make almanacs. Mathematics teach how to reckon interest, and, by the aid of chemistry, gunpowder, and shaving soap, and other such things have been invented or discovered.

What if this truth be not *the* truth to you? No matter! It is of no use to tell your truth, that knowledge, like virtue, is worth having for its own sake, rather than for the sake of its uses. They will not understand nor believe you. And yet, like the man born blind, who will not believe in nor understand light,

they are suffering for want of that in which·they dis-
believe.

They believe all these needs of which I have spoken,
to be only imaginary wants, and as for the imagination
itself, it is supposed to be too vague and unreal a thing
to have any real needs of its own.

Just what Jesus says we are to take no thought
for—" what we shall eat, and what we shall drink, and
wherewithal we shall be clothed," are the only things
we *do* take thought for and reckon valuable, except
money, that treasure we are warned *not* to lay up in
this rusty, moth-eaten, and thievish world.

"As a man thinketh, so is he." Our thoughts are
us. What we *think*, we *are*. What we *know*, we *are*.
What we learn becomes part of our minds. That
which we remember who shall teach us to forget? *Is*
death the everlasting sleep unbelievers teach? Do we,
Christians, *really believe* ourselves immortal? And if
we *do*, where are the treasures we are accumulating to
take with us into the safety of an incorruptible world?

We can take only ourselves along, without the
bodies of dust, and all the wealth we can take must be
part of ourselves.

Where is that wealth? We can carry the memory
of houses and lands, and food and raiment, with us, but
will these remembered riches make us rich in eternity?
Are they any element of true happiness here?

Answer, O Midas! starving at thy own golden
feast!

Will the memory of the giddy excitement of *mere*
amusements make a part of that wealth? How shall thy
dancing skill content thee, where feet dance no more?

Or how shall the ribald jest of the circus-clown, or the airy walk of the acrobat, reach, even in this world, to thy inner discontent, or appease its cry? And canst thou carry with thee, for a single hour, a serener tranquillity, for having seen centaurs at the hippodrome, or the dizzy gyrations of the puppets at the theatre? When the lights are out—when the dance is done—the play played out—what is there left but the dregs of petty jealousies, and envyings, and heart-burnings, with all the flavor and aroma of pleasure exhaled and gone?

The most candid of pleasure-seekers only claim for such things, the power of diverting for the time the painful or wearisome current of every day thoughts and feelings; or the office of filling up with its manufactured mirth and dazzle, the oft-recurring hiatus in life, which else would be empty and bare.

Amusements have no higher office than diversion; they never can be a true *interest* and *object* in anything worthy to be called life. And yet how many intellects have asked for bread, and had these stones given them! Whatever of value these things may have in their own place, they never can be satisfactorily substituted for the substance of worthier things.

But find a real interest in those strata of truths which lie below all the mud and soil of what is temporary and artificial, below the crust of conventionalism, or the quicksands of the relative and speculative, where men get lost as in a quagmire; ground your interest on what is positive and accessible, and life itself becomes a pleasure.

He who sups on sweets will find his mouth bitter in

the morning, but a simpler food will nourish without any after penalty; so if you gorge the mind, or its servant, the memory, with unsuitable diet, they will get a distaste for food from indigestion.

This state is worse than that of famine. It is not the stuffing process of the ordinary educational mills, called schools, which is to supply the wants of the hungry minds, supersede the vulgar and paltry amusements of the day, or overthrow the dynasty of the Blondins and Blitzes.

The ordinary educational programme is too much like a recipe in a cookery book, to be the thing needed. "A cup full of butter, a cup full of sugar, a cup full of flour, a cup full of cream, four eggs, a teaspoon full of soda, with salt and spice to your taste," is not a very essentially different prescription from, "A book full of geography, a book full of grammar, a book full of arithmetic, a book full of words to spell, an empty book to be filled with written words, a little composition, a little declamation, with singing to your taste."

To be satisfied with only this, would be as impossible as for the four years' old lad to love to go to school where his whole experience consisted in "sitting on a bench and saying A."

No traveller, however expeditious, ever expects to see all there is to be seen in the world. It is too much for him. Life is too short, and the world too long, for such an exploit. Neither does any person expect to learn all that there is to be learned in the realm of knowledge. A man who would try to farm a whole continent would have poor crops, but he who ploughs only so much as he can attend to, will have abundance.

One thing thoroughly done is worth more than many slighted jobs. One field of inquiry thoroughly explored, is better than a smattering knowledge of many.

There are two Grand Divisions in the world of Learning—the Temporary and the Immortal.

Of the Temporary are all manual Arts, all of the *this world* Literature which contains no essential and undying truth, all Languages which will be useless where the thoughts will use no syntax nor lexicon in their utterance. All these have a single attribute of immortality, for the discipline they give the mind, it retains, when the learning that made it strong and astute, becomes rubbish in that future life we are preparing for, where there will be no use for such knowledges.

The Immortal Learning is that which we can not only carry with us, but *use* in eternity. These are Positive or Absolute knowledges, those truths eternally true, demonstrable by plain proof, or immediately perceivable, things which can be reached without theory or guess work—the very bones and sinews of learning, the kernel of knowledge—the for ever satisfactory. In this realm, too, lies the border land between this world's knowings and the next, where the Philosophies dwell, like the angel of the Apocalypse, with one foot on the earth, and the other on the unseen sea.

Learning is not wisdom, nor is it always knowledge. It is not what is put into the mind, but what the mind is made capable of doing and producing, which is the desideratum.

Knowledge is mental food. The mind gets hungry for the aliment it digests and appropriates to grow strong upon, just as the body feels the want of physical nutriment.

Undigested food, either physical or mental, is useless and often detrimental.

Yet knowledge is worth having for its own sake—is worthy of love and effort for the sake of its own value. The pursuit of it is a keen pleasure, and its attainment a solid satisfaction.

Nothing is ever earnestly pursued for any sake but its own. If we, for a time, seek one thing for the sake of another, the pursuit is dropped when the object is gained, or when a shorter method of reaching it offers itself. A student may study for a diploma, and when he gets it, he forgets his wearisome learning, and takes to something he likes better. The man who stops his drams to win a wife, will take to his cups again when the foolish woman is caught; he did not love virtue for its own sake, but adopted it temporarily for another sake. The student who studies for the sake of the uses of knowledge may make a *good* scholar, but never a *great* one. All greatness must grow from an all-absorbing love for the object. The pursuit of the object becomes a passion, and the passion becomes exalted into devotion. Other considerations may be of importance, may be respected—attended to in a measure—loved second best—but the profoundest love is never forgotten, never neglected, never put off for minor things—and all other earthly things *are* minor in comparison with this.

Such devotion makes the great painter, the great musician, architect, or naturalist. The mere ordinary aimless aims of life are poor grovelling to them. The majority of people live because they were born, and have not died yet. They only live because they are alive, and do not know what else to do. Any vegetable does as much. But these others have ennobled life by their brave living. Most of us leave it ignoble enough, in our aimless twaddling which we accept as life. But try to bribe or threaten men or women who have some such object in existence—who live on purpose, and are glad they are alive—who would have chosen to be born if they had been consulted, and who live, even here, after they die. See what answer you will get of such!

The musician Haydn (I think it was) when threatened with what would be a terrible punishment to an ordinary artist—the condemnation of the popular school of music, which, they told him, forbade certain liberties which he had taken with the established rules. "But they are agreeable to the ear, and *I allow them!*" was the reply of this man, who loved his art better than he loved success. His great love conquered the arbitrary rule, and achieved success in the teeth of criticism.

"Do not paint, or you will starve!" said her friends to young Rosa Bonheur, "you shall be a milliner and get rich!" But the enthusiast loved art better than money or bread, and studied beasts in the dirty shambles, rather than laces and flowers in the shop, and through her severe and toilsome obedience to the one absorbing passion of her life, she conquered obstacles, and poverty, and prejudice, and stands crowned with wealth and honors among those who would have made her a milliner.

The Emperor of France offered the most honorable place and the highest salary offered to any Professor in his empire, to the Swiss naturalist, who replied that he

4*

had not time to attend to it. A *little* man would have had no time for anything else! "You shall have any price you ask, if you will but give us a lecture!" said a lyceum committee to the same great naturalist, but, "*I have no time to waste in making money!*" was the simply sublime reply of Agassiz.

Ah! such souls live in a clearer atmosphere than the dull fogs most of us inhabit. They reckon profit and loss by a different currency, and their riches cannot be computed in gold and silver.

They have loved their love *for its own sake.*

An ordinary conventional life is so hollow, that it will sound like an empty cask, when it comes in contact with what is substantial; but let this life grow as if it were alive, and be filled with substance, and it will no longer ring with its own emptiness.

There is no languor nor ennui to enervate the mind which has taken an earnest hold of the teachings of nature.

He who is intimate with nature at home cannot be ignorant, though he may never have learned the alphabet. He has the key to a realm of treasures of which nobody will dispute the possession, for, like language, it belongs to everybody who has a mind to use it.

It is a partly explored region, with new wonders waiting to be discovered by new adventurers, and exhaustless marvels for every explorer.

Happiness, with a vital zest and interest in it, abides out of doors with nature. You can find it there plenty and cheap. The birds and waters ask no admission tickets to their free concerts, and the miracles of growth and being, surpassing all the feats of all the magicians that ever lived, are there enacted every day.

Meet a man grievously vexed with the blue devils, and tell him there is an hour's serene happiness to be got out of a certain old crumbling mossy stump, surrounded by a sorrel sod and two dead mullein stalks, and he will think you are a fool, perhaps, and go on despising your childishness, and magnifying his own despair, because John Smith's note is worth only fifty cents on a dollar.

Never mind—you are a philosopher, and can afford to be thought a fool. Why not? If it is any comfort to any care-harassed mortal to set you down among the dunces, because you are not also tormented, let him have all the poor mite of satisfaction he can get out of a conviction of your stupidity. You live at headquarters, where happiness grows spontaneously with the weeds, and you can spare such bits of pleasure to anybody.

These poor mammon-ridden wretches would, perhaps, none of them be willing to have this persecuting Old Man of the Sea, of their cares, taken off their galled shoulders, to be exchanged for the thriftless joys of the naturalist.

As soon as you begin to enter into the arcana of nature, you feel the shackles of outward customs grow loose, and the liveries of many servitudes drop off, as a bird moults its feathers. Nothing is done suddenly, for Nature has plenty of time—all the time there is—and is never in a hurry. So these relics of old bondages wear out, and fall away piecemeal, and you hardly know when you lose them, but some day perhaps others tell you they are gone. They are finding fault as they tell you, and you know they tell the truth, because the complaint

does not annoy you as it would have done once. Other
men's opinions of you are now of less import to you
than your own. You respect yourself—you approve
yourself, therefore you can afford to be censured for
what is best and bravest in you—you can afford to be
misunderstood. What matter if even your friends
accuse you of growing "eccentric" on purpose to gain
the notice of other people's eyes! You can afford even
that, for you know that very unlike causes produce like
results, and forgetting that other people have eyes or
tongues, sometimes produces similar effects to remem-
bering those same eyes all the time. Human vanity
will permit but few persons to believe that their opinions
are matters of absolute indifference to one of their fellow mortals. They can understand how a person might
make himself ridiculous for the sake of being noticed,
but that that notice should be entirely forgotten and
unthought of is inconceivable!

Let them flatter themselves that they have demo-
lished you by their ridicule. If it pleases them there
is that much pleasure gained to the world, and as you
have not felt it, you have lost nothing.

You have changed your standard of measurement.
You no longer ask; "Do they believe it?" but, "Is it
right in itself?" This return to the normal standard—
to the absolute truth instead of the accepted version of
things, will work great transformations in any character, definite enough to deserve the name of character.

Unnoticed as the process of liberation may be, the
effect of the liberty is noticeable enough. A prisoner,
long in shackles, when first released, still walks as if

restrained; but the artificial gait soon wears out, and liberty restores the grace of unfettered motion.

In the woods and fields, people's eyes are off, and you who had been a prisoner to their criticisms, find your limbs loose and you walk freely. By and by you get the habit of being free, even among your fellows. They were your jailors once, but their term of office has expired for ever.

Of course those people to whom liberty is offensive, will find fault. They will sneer at, and perhaps slander you. What if they do? It is their bent—let them have it! (Especially as you cannot hinder them.)

If they were in China they would be shocked at a woman's foot if it took the liberty of growing as God intended. If they lived in Malacca they would be disgusted with any man who would dare to let his teeth remain "white like a dog's." If they were among our aborigines they would be scandalized at the bad taste of any military gentleman who would prefer his own unstained complexion to the fashionable bars of red and black paint, with which their code of decorum insists they should beautify their countenances.

Of course Fashion will be against you, but what of it? Counting numbers, you will be in a very small minority; but in very truth, where is the majority greater than your Liberty, Nature, and Nature's God?

Mental liberty is a prerequisite to all deep and abiding happiness, and Nature sets you free, if you are willing to be emancipated.

When you have achieved sufficient independence to be able to make your own observations, from thence do your own reasoning, and deduce your own conclusions

with tolerable accuracy, you are just prepared to com-
mence those explorations that none have achieved before
you, and that the scientific world is waiting for. Why
should not you, as well as another, unlock those mysteries, and enrich mankind with new revelations of
science ?

There are momentous problems, as well as less significant ones, waiting for solution. A few examples of
these unsolved problems will convince the dullest
believer in plodding stupidity, that there are at least a
few scientific facts worth discovering.

Over a large tract of our Western country, there
prevails at a certain season of the year, a strange and
often fatal disease among cattle, known as the milk sickness. It is evidently produced by poison, and the
poison-producing tracts are so definitely marked that
they can be fenced in, and the cattle kept out, and the
disease ceases. But though this disease is so wide
spread and so well known when it appears, and its
locality so plainly discoverable, no one has yet been able,
with any reasonable show of demonstration, to tell the
cause of this remarkable fatality. The inclosed noxious
localities have been examined, inch by inch, for they
are generally quite limited in extent, and yet nothing
has been discovered there, not common to all the rest
of the region round about.

Now the stupidest Hoosier that ever thought "larnin'"
a humbug, would be glad to know the cause of this
plague, especially if, as is often the case, the knowledge
of the cause would indicate the kind of remedy needed.

In this case superficial and unphilosophical investiga-
tions have proved to be worthless. The only index to

the probable cause, yet found, is the declarations of the only men of science who have looked into it. These are physicians, who declare the disease to have every appearance of being produced by a mineral poison. The farmers, who had before convinced themselves that if it was produced by any vegetable agent, it was an invisible one, ploughed up and examined the plague spots, without result. There were no chemists among them to test the soil, nor explorers to investigate the wherefore of those mineral exhalations, if such they were, making their appearance at one season more than another.

This problem, of pecuniary and sanitary as well as scientific interest, remains to be solved.

When will some naturalist give us the *modus operandi* of the fungus called smut, in grain, and discover its remedy?

Who will demonstrate the cause of the potato disease, and devise a preventive?

A reasonable acquaintance with natural science would prevent some disastrous mistakes. Men have beggared themselves in search of coal and other minerals, in places where any tolerable geologist could have foretold certain failure, since he would know that such minerals are *never* found in such places.

I cite these few examples from multitudes I might mention, to show that mere utilitarians, of the coarsest type, have a bread and butter interest in the growth of scientific knowledge, and that the ploddingest plodders will gain a dollar and cent advantage from the researches of those whose thriftless studies they could see no use in.

Thinkers will see that the far better and truer reasons for the study of Nature, I have given first.

"This is all very well," says one, "for those who have time to attend to it, but working people have no time for such studies."

Let us look at this excuse for a moment.

We do not expect a woman who does her own housework, and sewing for a husband and seven children, beside workmen and boarders, to be very much at leisure for intellectual pursuits, nor would we expect to find a devotee of science in a man with a sick wife and innumerable responsibilities, little and great, to provide for. The mere fact that such people contrive to live *at all*, proves how much can be got out of twenty-four hours per day.

See how many useless and foolish things get done, and reckon if the useful and healthful pursuit of knowledge would not occupy the same time far more pleasantly and profitably.

When we, the working people, make such excuses for ourselves, we justify the insolent effrontery of those aristocrats who claim that it is necessary to have a privileged class to do the learning and thinking, leaving another class to perform all labor; for labor, they say, is incompatible with study and thought. Indignant denials of our inferiority are only ridiculous, when *we* declare ourselves to be unable to make ourselves the peers of any class we please.

Have you forgotten Hugh Miller, the Scotch quarryman's apprentice, who studied the revelations Nature made to him in his vocation, and thus became the world-renowned geologist? He tells not only the result, but the process of his learning, and shows how his love of knowledge was a perennial enjoyment and blessing to him—a safeguard against the seductions of vice and extravagance—an incentive to industry and virtue—and, though he does not say it, we know it was a rich gift to the world.

Indeed his whole career goes to show that physical labor is a help to mental growth and health, for when the growing importance of his intellectual labors and discoveries caused him to devote himself exclusively to study, abandoning the manual labor of his earlier years, the overtaxed mind gave way, and the man went mad and died.

The nice balance of the physical and mental forces was lost, and all was lost. His greatness grew out of his using his mind and his hands in connexion.

Any farmer's boy or girl has as much opportunity as he, and as much time. He observed as he worked. So can any of us who live in the country. We can study Nature as we work in the garden and the field. What few books we need, cost less than we expend for the so-called pleasures of which I have spoken.

We afford those things we care most for. If we care most for dress and show, we will find ways to afford aliment for our vanity. If we care most for money we will contrive to accumulate it. If we care most for the opinions of others, we will devote time and energy to winning their favor. If we love moral and spiritual things best, we will not stint our devotions and our souls' culture to a few hours on Sunday. If we care more for our minds than our bodies, our minds will be ministered to. If we choose, we may be learned and even wise.

Nature is not an exacting mistress. She will yield her treasures to one who gives her only the odd scraps of half worn hours, and the fag end of holidays. She is patient, and for ever new. To the weary and heart-worn, or to the empty soul, she is an untiring solace—a faithful friend. Her lessons are food and rest, and like a fountain in a desert place, or "the shadow of a great rock in a weary land."

In our often arbitrary use of the terms "good" and "bad," "perfect" and "imperfect," we betray a faith, instinctive and unconquerable, in the existence of a positive standard of perfection, to or from which all our comparisons are made.

If beauty or goodness were but comparative qualities, our language would not need, and never would have had a superlative form of expression. But the simple fact that mankind, even in the earlier ages, felt the necessity of some mode of expressing the different degrees of excellence, from a lower up to a higher, and *the highest*, shows the existence of a common instinct of the race recognising the ideal of the perfect, and the aspirations of mankind have ever been directed towards this ideal.

Slowly, as through the lapse of ages Truth fed the hungry multitude by the hands of her chosen philosophers and prophets, has the world recognised a nearer approach to the absolute standard.

The soul of Nature stretches out her hands in her great yearning towards the better and the higher, and though in her eagerness she grasps too often a spurious good—a delusive shadow of better things—still, though cheated and mistaken, and crowned with a thorny and stinging experience, her hunger and thirst after perfection proves the existence of a supply suited to her wants.

Nowhere in God's universe is there any natural want given, without a suitable supply, prepared somewhere in nature, to meet it. The lips and speech—the ear and sound—the eye and light—the heaving lungs and the inbreathed air, in their adaptation to each other are but a few from myriads of examples and proofs of this truth.

Nature is young yet, with childhood's instinctive unrest and foreknowledge of its own predestined growth and maturity, and though her hopes are sometimes wild and extravagant, the slow coming perfection of her life shall as far exceed her present ideal, as the realities of life transcend the visionary castles in the air built for its future by the child.

Begin where we will, in the lower, material world, we find this same tendency from a lower towards a higher; we find that there exists an ideal type of perfection for every grade of being.

From the slippery mud that clogs our wagon wheels, and scarce serves to make the commonest brick, through the finer material of which the chemist forms his crucible, and that which the potter moulds into shapes to suit his will, to that highest type of argillaceous existence—the porcelain clay, which labor and fire transform into creations of such beauty, that human pride loves to add them to its stores of brittle magnificence.

From the yellow-grey desert sand, to the crystal and stores of gems,—from dingy charcoal dust, to diamond sparks and the "mountain of light" to which Brahmins paid divine honors.

From the lime we plaster on our walls, up through the rich marbles and alabaster—that build fountains and tombs—palaces and monuments, and growing life-like under the sculptor's hands, give down from age to age the artist's ideas of physical perfection. Through the strange machinery of animal skeletons, and the varying beauty of many-tinted shells to the coral trees growing with the instinct of animal life, working and breathing, as it builds island walls from old ocean's floor up to the sunlight.

From all of these advances towards perfection among existences below consciousness or volition, we infer inevitably the progress of the very elements themselves, towards the most perfect development possible to their natures; and the continued transition from the mineral to the vegetable and animal kingdoms, by becoming aliment to supply some of their needs in the mysterious process of nutrition and growth, evinces a tendency in lower to grow up and pass into higher states of existence.

The miracle of Adam's creation from the dust of the earth is renewed in the growth of every living creature, since the earth and the elements are converted in the laboratory of vegetable existences, into the food which is again transformed, in the alembic of the body, into materials for forming the body itself. Like Adam, every man is made of dust.

This great sermon on the transfiguration of matter, preached by the stones during all the six thousand years of man's existence, has been heard in different ages, by different disciples of nature, who, while accepting the outward truth so far as they understood it, gave always some mythical and hidden significance to the plain speech of their teacher, evolving by the magic of poetry, from stubborn facts, beautiful fictitious theories by which to solve eternity's problem of the origin, the existence and the destiny of spirit.

Mrs. Child brings up the old idea of the growth of spirit out of matter, or rather its growth *through* matter, in her "Poet's dream of the soul," in which she represents an agate lying in the earth, gaining the sole idea of its existence from the roots of a violet which embraced it. The knowledge that there was such a thing as life filled the stone with so intense a desire for an existence having an element of vitality—life—that it wished itself away into a lichen that grew up in the sunshine and felt the inspiration of the winds of heaven. But that aspiration which belongs to spirit, and seems even to impel upwards insensate matter, stirred in the new existence of that spark of spiritual life, and as it learned of higher forms of being—higher grades and developments in life, again it passed upwards into a higher sphere, and again, and yet again, until through varied shapes it passed through a nightingale into the musician Mendelssohn.

This poetical fiction was once accepted by a school of philosophers, who certainly had more foundation for their theory than many another school and sect, which have obtained more widely in the world than this, for though these men took the shadow for the substance, still there *was a substance* to cast the shadow, while many a school of sectaries have built their faith on the "shadow of a shade."

But to return from this speculative soul-making to the passing of the mineral up into the vegetable kingdom, and there trace the footprints of nature's upward pilgrimage, from the first initial Algæ of Geologic revelation, to the elaborately perfected Phænogamia of the historic period. We find in those vast fossil forests revealed to us in coal beds, mostly gigantic Cryptogamia, luxuriant and wonderful, yet lacking many of the organs common to all the more perfectly organized plants, of our present more diminutive, but more numerous, and more highly finished genera of plants.

But beyond this passing from one species of an earlier period to a more perfect one of a later, there is this perfecting process going on in the different varieties of the same species, under favorable circumstances many varieties being coined at will by the ingenuity and skill of the human race. Thus a single variety of wild rose, perfect in itself, in one sense of the word perfect, can be varied by climate, and soil, and cultivation, into innumerable phases of beauty, " differing one from the other as the stars differ in glory," yet all developments of the ideal perfection, which, though absolute and infinite, admits of more variation than imperfection, which is comparative and limited.

Naturalists tell us that double flowers are monsters ; but the universal consent of all tastes, civilized and savage, has pronounced this development of educated nature to be beautiful, and thus contradicts the idea of deformity which is always hideous.

The wild crab tree was perfect as a crab, but not as an apple, until its wild bitterness was won away by the faithful and kind education given it by those it so plenteously rewarded with the luscious richness of its harvest gifts.

Some of the higher orders of plants seem to be

endowed, not only with sensation, but with instinct, discovering by some unknown power, the presence of various substances not in actual contact with them. Thus several species of vines, such as pumpkins and melons, will in one night turn the straightforward direction of their growth to reach a vessel of water placed a few inches to one side of their path. Twining plants will reach a support placed near them, and tendrils remain uncurled, stretching out their long fingers to find something they can cling to, which, when found, they lose no time in grasping.

The Dionea sets snares for the luckless flies it lures with its sweetness, and then, like a spider or a coquette, imprisons and pierces its victims with its thorns; and these insects are said to supply an important item of food to this carnivorous vegetable. The pitcher plant in the desert, opens and holds up its cruse to catch the rain and dew, and then shuts down its lid to keep the sun from stealing away the treasure. The mimosa, most like an animal of all, shrinks from a touch, and even dies to escape the cruel handling of those who wish to gratify their curiosity at the expense of its sensitive organism.

All these approaches towards sensation and volition, betoken advancement towards the object of nature's involuntary yet incessant search—*a something higher*. But as we seldom find the realization of our expectations in the place or manner we had calculated on, so if we look among these higher developments of plant life for the place where the vegetable kingdom is to be found in nearest approximation towards the animal, we shall not find it. The bottom of the valley of humiliation is the nearest place to Heaven, so among the lower Algæ, the very alpha of vegetation, we are to look for those strange animal plants, or vegetable animals, which link the two kingdoms together and make their boundary lines indefinite. From these the transition is rapid to the zoophytes, and up, through an almost endless chain of marine and terrestrial animals, whose cold, and often colorless, blood seems as lifeless as the sap of trees, or the crimson juice of the bleeding sanguinaria.

But the organism that approaches nearer and nearer the perfect, not only through all the successive Geologic periods, but up from one race to another of existing animals, develops more and more of that species of intelligence called instinct, until the more fervent action of the vital forces brings warmth, and dawning glimpses of intellect, which, growing finer and purer, less gross and more flexible, becomes complicated—active with the impulses of will, and the teachings of something very like reason, if not its very self, until it emerges from this long, long line of successive, ever-advancing existences, into the highest type of animal existences yet known—the Human.

When we come to the more perfectly organized plants and animals we find a new and important feature developing itself, and this is the more *distinct individuality* of the single members of any species. Hitherto we have been considering differences shaded off into almost indistinguishable likenesses, and diversities becoming apparently identical. From considering these seeming transitions, and likenesses between differences, we turn to scanning those yet stranger individual distinctions which separate the universe into items which must for ever remain distinct. Among many plants, copies of original varieties can only be obtained by grafting, budding, cuttings, &c., the *seed* producing new individual varieties endlessly; but when we come to animals, this exceptional mode of producing synonyms no longer exists, and we can find only individuals, in a great measure resembling each other, it is true, but in the superior races, so essentially differing in character, as to require separate study to understand the treatment of each individual, in place of the generalizing process which sufficed with plants and the lower animals.

This individuality, in some degree, exists among all organized beings, and in each individual can be clearly, definitely, and easily traced, the advancing steps of nature towards perfection. In plants—even in the simplest and lowest, the individual can be traced from the minute spore or seed, through the various stages of germination and growth—its first singular leaves, and after growth of foliage, its blossoming and fruitage, and until the ascending circle is completed in the seed containing the life of another generation.

The lower animals, like plants, change more externally than those of a higher order.

Thus the mosquito passes from its egg-built life-boat into a water monster of minute dimensions, and afterwards leaving the skin which protected its aquatic existence as a legacy to its native puddle, it creeps into upper air, furnished with wings and a song. Numerous reptiles perform this pilgrimage through two elements in order to perfect their natural developments, and the whole or nearly the whole tribe of winged insects undergo the change from creeping to flying things. Some of these transformations are so beautiful as to be assumed as types of mankind's angel life, following the human one.

The Greeks carved butterflies on their tombstones as emblems of the changed condition of the individual whose forsaken shell lay under the monument.

The larvæ, emerging from the egg's prison shell, and crawling, dim-sighted and slow, as it grew to the full size and perfection of its worm-life, feels the hour approaching when the caterpillar must die and the butterfly be born ; so, sometimes winding itself in a silken shroud, and sometimes casing itself in a hard horny shell, it falls into a sleep from which it awakes not a blind, trailing worm, but a new creature, many-eyed and rainbow-winged, no longer doomed to gnaw its daily food from bitter leaves, but to float ever among flowers, and drink their full cups of sweetness.

Of all the emblems of the myth-loving Greeks, I know of none so beautiful as this type of growth from the low and loathsome to the perfected and beautiful individual creature.

From the bare nestling, with its great head, and sealed eyes, and its wide gaping mouth, through the chirping fledgling, to the full plumed singing bird, as from the babe through childhood and youth to the full grown adult, we see always before us the operation of the same universal law of progress, the same tendency in the natural to perfect itself.

Thus far have we traced the material, visible, tangible revelations of Nature, and their unvarying teachings point us forward and upward. She has qualities which we are too little and too ignorant to weigh or measure, properties as undeniable as they are incomprehensible and inscrutable. But no one of them contradicts this one great lesson; though we do not know positively that they have been subject to this progressive law, neither do we know the contrary.

Light may be precisely as it has always been since its creation, but not *where* it has always been, for it is ever moving, ever fleeing through space, like a thought, to reach some more distant spot in the universe.

Heat, too, may be an eternal element, changeless and perfect from the beginning; but if electricity has, we have no evidence of the fact, for its phenomena have progressed essentially since the scientific observations of men were first recorded. It is not yet three hundred years, I believe, since the Aurora Borealis, generally believed to be an electric phenomenon, was first observed. If it had existed prior to that time, as it now exists, people could not fail to observe it, and a people superstitious enough to be frightened out of their wits by a comet, would surely have as well recorded their terror at a sky all ablaze with strange cold flames, such as light some of our winter nights, as to have written down their exorcisms of Satan in order to light the darkness of an eclipse.

History and analogy, then, go to teach us that universal nature is, and ever has been, climbing upwards towards perfection. True, all organized being is reducible to a few simple elements, in which there is no such law apparent; yet these elements seem restlessly seeking to enter new combinations, and in these combinations to become part of new organizations, and there obey this organic law of the universe.

In following the material creation up from its inau-

guration, we come to places where were successively
developed animation, volition, will, intelligence, and
reason, all of which, except the first, find their highest
development in the Human race. All the passions,
feelings, and most of the instincts of the lower animals,
are heightened, spiritualized, and intensified, and form
an essential part of the invisible man; and these faculties, or rather feelings, seem, when we find them in their
less perverted and more natural state, like all lesser
things, to recognise the existence of a higher life, and
by their endeavor to slough off their unnatural corrup-
tion and depravity, seek to assimilate themselves to their
ideal type of natural perfection.

All the intelligence and reason of the lower animals
find a deeper, stronger, more elevated, and very much
more extensive and perfect development in the intellect
of man, and this superiority of a force, stronger than
the physical, is acknowledged by the lower races. The
hyena and tiger quail before the steady gaze of a soul-
lighted eye, and the hungriest bear will not devour the
child who fixes its eye-balls on his own.

But it is not the supremacy of the intellect alone
which gives the human will its power over the brute.
In him there is made manifest a new faculty or force,
not demonstrated to exist in any other animal—the
beginning, the initial, the alpha, the algæ and zoophyte
of a new ascending series of being—winding its spiral
circles above him, through angel and archangel, seraph
and cherub, up to the All-Beautiful, All-Wise, All-Good,
All-Powerful, Essential and Eternal Spirit of the universe.

The existence of this ascending series of being, beyond

the point where it sojourns in the flesh, because inaudible, invisible, and intangible to the senses, has been doubted by some who believed that nature was perfected in man—that he was the ultimate, the highest—and that the perfection of the natural was limited to man's capacity for improvement and perfection. But this class of persons has always been, and probably always will be, few in number and limited in influence, for in man, as in all the rest of nature, only more self-conscious and positive, heave and throb those irresistible "propulsions from the night," which never move idly towards nothing, but always directly in obedience to the strong upward attraction of higher forces.

Does the restless tide disturb the great deep in idle wantonness, or because the resistless attraction of an upper world woos it to follow its aspirations? Why then, think ye, should the great tide-wave of human aspirations after the higher and holier existences, be called the aimless heaving of native unrest?

This restless, far-reaching instinct of the soul aspiring towards its ideal, is our best and highest proof of the existence, and the best demonstration of the nature of the unknown world to which we are hastening, and of the beings inhabiting it, as well as of our own immortality.

That God made man in His own image, we all prove by constantly inverting the process, and making Him in the image of our inner selves. Every sort of man makes his ideal deity something like himself—fashions him according to his own ideas of perfection; so we find the general ideas of God exceedingly diversified and contradictory, as well as indefinite and confused. The man only a little abovo the beasts has a strong, passionate, wilful Deity as his mind's ideal—the cruel man has his Vengeance and Terror God, and the beast man worships his crocodiles. Adam, in his ignorance, imagined the Creator to be as gullible as himself, and sought to hide from his presence. Some philosophers and many poets, supposing their faculties to have each their prototype in a separate divine existence, based on man's multifold nature strange systems of polytheism. Others supposed all the sinless universe to be pervaded by an essence they called God. But the sensual represented their god as a devil; and the philosophers described a "keen, cold" matchless intellect as their deity; a set of weaker heads and warmer hearts learned God's diviner attributes of justice, mercy, and love. Afterwards—ascending ever—prophets with both heads and hearts, learned and taught how the manifold manifestations of God were only parts of a whole—how the all-pervading Life Essence, and the guiding Intelligence, and the Spirit of love and compassion, were all but parts of the Great First Cause.

Slowly and vaguely, dimly and indistinctly dawned these successive ideas on the world, and came at last to assume a character for Deity which was the immutable and absolute right—the abstract Spirit and concrete Essence of perfection—the ultimatum of the universe. But men differ so widely in their notions of right that their ideas of God are as diversified as ever, for there are those of every grade of worshippers known in any age, still living and worshipping their highest idea of the good and true, from the votaries of serpent gods to the disciples of the Universal Heart.

But God, not being limited by man's base ideas of

him, has so ordained His laws, or they so exist in Him
as a part of himself, that they can nowhere be trans-
gressed with impunity, thus fixing limits and boundaries
to right and wrong, making truth an absolute and positive thing—a real, demonstrable fact in existence—so
that man has but to read nature's open scroll, to learn
the truths it behoves him to know.

But nature's scroll is a sealed book to most eyes—a
chart of life's voyage made out in unintelligible hiero-
glyphics, which men are too lazy or too stupid to learn,
hence the blind groping of the race for ages to find the
way of truth, to which every tree pointed with innumerable fingers, of which every brook babbled, and every
breeze whispered—the thunder pealed out the lesson,
and the birds warbled it everywhere—the mute flowers
breathed it out in odorous sighs, and the heart of man
echoed the voices, yet lost the meaning of his teachers.

Other revelations were given, but the burning
truths that came from the inspired lips of God's chosen,
fell on the same dull ears and clouded understandings,
till their divine harmonies were tortured into discord,
and men learned but disjointed scraps of the great
truth.

But as " Chaos and old night" faded and dissolved
before the light and life of creation, so pass away these
dark and cloudy troubles from the human soul. Slowly
do the dull ears and duller understandings of men come
to hear and understand the demonstration of truth's
absolute law, and more slowly still do they come to
yield it obedience,—*but they are moving !*

But heavily and slowly, like blind Orion climbing up
the mountain, bearing his guide up the steep to the

summit, where he might meet the first rays of the morning's sunlight, which were to unseal his closed lids, so climbs the great world, burdened and blind, towards the all-revealing future. The past clings like tendrilled vines, or thorny and hooked-fingered brambles, to her wet trailing garments, and holds and hinders her from moving on, since she knows not the pathway, and her guides are almost, or quite, as blind as she.

In the many-voiced chorus of the by-gone, she seldom heeds or hears the tones of prophecy and "lofty cheer," but listens, with flagging steps and weary heart, to the oft-recurring refrain, "Tempt not the untried ill in search of the unknown good—keep what thou hast—it is thine"—and were it not for the restless life-growth in all things, the world, obedient to its conservative teachers, would stagnate and die.

This world-growth may be likened unto a handful of acorns cast on the earth, and one of them felt the sunshine and the dew, and received them as coming from Heaven, and her heart swelled within her till the smooth hard prison-house that held it, burst apart with the power of the life that was in it. And then the conservative acorns around it began to cry out, "O foolish acorn! when Heaven gave thee so smooth and beautiful a shell to protect thee from the cold rain and withering sunshine, why wilt thou ungratefully despise its gifts, and choose these restless elements for thy companions, when they will certainly destroy thee? A while ago thou wast an acorn, but now thou art nothing but a misshapen mass of fermenting material."

But the acorn felt the inspiration of life, and answered, as inspired enthusiasts always answer, in a language her

5*

sisters could not understand—and they chid her, as one gone mad.

But after a time, she stretched out her hands so far to embrace the free air, that her two first leaves, all wrinkled and ridged, spread out in the sunshine, and her feet clung closely to the moist earth, and she stood, a living, growing thing.

And her sisters said, " Who would think that nonde-script, bold green monster, staring in the face of the sun, had ever been a beautiful white acorn, modestly folded in her brown house? But she will soon reap the reward of her temerity, for one baby footstep would crush her to pieces now, while we are as safe as ever."

But the young plant felt her soul swell with more life, and as she looked up to the quiet stars beckoning above, her heart opened, and began to put forth a new leaf—thinner, and wider, and deeper colored than the first; and she rejoiced—for growth was so happy, and so glorious! But when her sleepy sisters awoke in the morning, and saw her again expanded and changed, they cried out the more exceedingly against her, for her fickleness, and told her to behold how constant *they* were to first principles and old truths. But as the plant grew, neither by creed nor theory, nor even by reason, but by instinct, and inspiration, and necessity, she was "grieved in her heart," and having no cavilling sophistry where-with to answer their stereotyped logic, and the living words of truth "being as foolishness" in their ears, she grew on and " answered not a word."

But when the Summer was ended and Autumn came and painted the green leaf red, and took away the first pair, the sisters said, " Behold! she is dying! The frost cuts through her flimsy foliage, and destroys her, but we are snug and safe where nature put us, and defy the storms. Let us take warning by her folly, and be contended with our condition." But the young oak cried out earnestly, that nature meant she should grow, or she would not have given her the power, and that she should not die but live. And they said, "Then was it intended that man should sin, or he would not have had the ability!" and they laughed her to scorn.

Then the snow came, and they slept.

But when the "Winter was over and gone," and Spring filled the oak with fresh vigor, it branched and spread, and grew and thrived luxuriantly, and the fault-finding acorns grew silent, or only grumbled in whispers; but afterwards when the oak found honor, and the acorns were unnoticed, they began to envy their sister, and take pride in her, and try to imitate her, but decay had fixed upon them, and worms gnawed into them, and they learned, too late, that when nature bestowed sunshine and rain, she meant they should be used, as well as her temporary sheltering gift of shells.

So the human part of the natural world, like the life-inspired acorn, shall grow in spite of sneers and cavil—in spite of frost and storm, of time and delay—and become beautiful and glorious, even as the oak became monarch of the forest.

Men have already begun to listen for the true teachings of the great Past, which stands, sybil-like, chanting her oracle and prophecies, and pointing to the records of her progressive march, graven on all the rocks adown the stream of time.

To those who have learned to hear aright, her song

teaches us to struggle upwards towards the future, as she struggled to reach the present, ever nearing that great object of her search and ours—the highest ideal—the truest truth—the ultimate perfection.

The poet tells us that

> "There is a mighty chain of being
> Lessening down, from Infinite perfection
> To the brink of dreary nothing"—

and it is true. The converse of it is also true, and we are tending upwards in the ascending scale, enlarging and growing, from the atom up to Deity, and when the struggle shall cease, and that harmonious march up towards the infinite—that march which is to be trodden through eternity, to the music of the spheres, shall be begun, then shall each item of the universe in the perfection of its own nature

> "Be one with God, and God is All in All."

A PILGRIM PAGAN.

The dusky twilight of all time had come,
Earth's long and stormy day was closing fast,
And night, not earth-born like all other nights,
But born of space as stars are, swallowed up
The lingering relics of the by-gone light.
The Norsemen's fabled Raggnarokk had come,
When all the Gods of earth were to be judged
And swept away, and only " He whose name
No man dare utter," should be Lord of all.
And he, the fiery king of endless life,
Judged the pale spectres of the waning world.

" Come forth!" said the Eternal: from the tomb
The long dead Ages started back to life,
And bursting through the mould and dust of death,
Rehearsed the deeds of every by-gone day.

Thus witnessed one before that awful court:

There have been Angels, tho' in various guise,
From the beginning through the lapse of time;
Each martyr'd in his turn a thousand ways,
Each burthened with a host of evil names,
And scourged, and mocked, and cast aside in scorn,
Trampled and hated; yet 'twas marvel strange
That while the Angels thus were buffeted,
They each had altars whereon incense burned,

And they, the buffeters, sung psalms of praise,
And offered incense to the names of those
Whose incarnations they despised and slew.

The Angel, Truth, had temples old and new,
And throngs of worshippers bowed to her name ;
And yet the very temple's selves—their pomp
Of marble colonnade, and fretted roof,
Gold-gleaming spire, rare woods of distant climes,
And costly deckings—were but wooden cheats,
Poor, painted make-believes, whose honest cracks
Showed the plain pine beneath the rosewood lie
And rich mahogany falsehood, deftly told
By cunning workmen and their pots of paint.

This shabby showroom of men's vanities,
In solemn mockery named the House of Truth,
Was filled to flooding with a motley throng,
Who went—because it was the day to go—
Because it was the custom of the place—
Because the bell rung, and their clothes were on,
And folks would notice if they didn't go,
And folks would see their finery if they did.

Rolled thro' the vaulted roof the organ's peal,
And the sweet chant of voices in the choir:
The hymn once uttered by some earnest soul
Enhedged in darkness, seeking for the light,
Was chanted parrot-like by choral bands,
Who lost the meaning in the silv'ry sound.
Thus ran the burden of the solemn song:

All art Thou, but we are nothing,
    Help us, Oh! thou Truth sublime!
We are false, but Thou art faithful,
    Teach us all Thyself divine!

Wait we mourning round thy altars,
    For the life that Thou dost give,
Take our broken hearts and heal them!
    All our worthless gifts receive!

Followed the prayer in measured accents doled,
And sermon, tedious as an oft-told tale,
And then a pause. In thro' the outer door,
There passed a being most serene and calm,
And stood before the altar in the aisle,
And thus he spoke :—" Oh! fellow worshippers!
I come from a far realm away to join
The congregation of the friends of Truth,
Who has no temples in the land I left.

" There is within me that which turns from wrong,
Which shrinks from treach'rous deeds and lying lips,
An outgrowth unto all sincerity—
And with such aspirations as shall grow
To deeds, my spirit searches for the Truth—
The infinite—unfailing—utmost truth!
Enrol my name among the names of those
Who seek in her the ever highest good."

He paused, and ladies smiled behind their fans,
To think that such a funny looking man,

With such queer clothes as this strange pilgrim wore,
Should make a speech like that, so out of place,
When no one asked him, and none other spoke.
Could he not wait till the appointed time
For offering names ?   And then he could have made
A speech, and worn a garb, more à-la-mode.

The men drew down the corners of their mouths,
And looked half sneering towards their shining boots,
And wondered what the stranger's business was,
That would allow him to afford to be
So very much in love with thriftless Truth.

A few, more zealous than the rest, were glad—
Some that the neighboring temples all would gaze
With envious admiration on this new
Converted heathen, that none other had,
But was a unique feather in their cap.
Some liked his eloquence, and some were pleased
To hear their language with strange accent mouthed
In voice so musical by mouth so fine ;
And some were glad that their monotonous lives
Had had at last an interesting break,
And their stale gossip a fresh flavoring spice
For the next week at least.   But there were some,
" A beggarly account" of "nobodies,"
'Tis true, yet still a living few, whose hearts
Were thrilled with deeper joy than tongue may speak,
That there was one in all the earth to dare
Exile and ridicule for Truth's dear sake. ·

Then spoke the minister : " If you have read
Our Articles of Faith, and can confess

The Creed and Catechism without flaw,
After initial rites, if none dissent,
We will admit you to our loving band."

The half-converted pagan looked aghast!
"I never heard of all the things you name,
Nor can conceive of an initial rite
Would make me love Truth more than I do now!"

"'Tis not for that," replied the minister,
"'Tis but a form of setting you apart
From all the world that does not follow Truth,
I will repeat the creed to you, and if
You can confess it afterward, 'tis done,
Say, 'I believe in Truth, the pure, the whole,
That she hath many eyes that she may see
All that exists; some scanning up, some down,
And some the limitless expanse between,
And hath as many tongues to speak of all
That she beholdeth in the universe,'
Can you repeat thus much?"
                    "And why should I?
For I know naught of this, and how believe?
It matters nothing to my love, if Truth
Hath but one eye, or two, or scores of them,
So that she still be Truth.   Why should I care?
She may be many tongued, for aught I know;
I would she had ten thousand living tongues
To speak in all the earth, and thus cry down
The clamorous lies with which the welkin rings.
I would exult in such triumphal song,
But I will listen with love's keenest ear,
In every tempest lull of falsehood's storm,

For the deep whispers of her still, small voice,
When she is bidden not to speak at all ;
And when men make it crime to speak her words,
Then will I speak them faithfully as now—
Will wear her badge when 'tis a badge of shame
And honor her thro' sneers and bitter scorn,
And tho' I have not numbered all her tongues,
I love and I believe in utmost Truth—
Pass by the rest, I cannot say it now !"

" But 'tis essential that you should *believe*,
And if 'tis ignorance that makes you halt
Become enlightened 'ere you seek to pass
The sacred pale of our especial Truth,
Outside of which all other Truths are vain !"

" I know," the heathen said, " I must have all,
That one great central part of Truth withdrawn
Will make all others seem but partial truths,
And half-truths are part falsehoods at the best,
I want the whole, what is entire, alive,
Breathing and throbbing, quick and warm with life,
A dead Truth is as worthless as a lie ;
If I take verity at second hand,
And say 'tis so, because *you* say 'tis so,
What is it better than dead truth to me ?
A falsehood were as quickening to the soul !"

" But you want Faith to guide where knowledge fails
We must believe those things we cannot know."

Slowly the puzzled heathen turned away,
And stood alone beneath the endless sky,

Baffled of human aid he must toil on,
And slowly proving all things, hold the good,
The good *alone*, against the faithless world.
The garb those sneering saints had thought so odd
Around his great, true heart he wrapped, and thus
Unto his inmost soul the hero spoke :

"Without conditions will I come to thee,
Thou all pervading Soul! The cumb'rous creed—
The cramping rite—the mouthing of strange words—
I leave for those who find a use for them,
But Thou, whose speech the soul can understand,
In the dead silence of the voiceless night,
Thy words come to my feverish soul as rain
Comes dropping on the dust-encumbered grass,
And freshens all its wilting stems and leaves
With its cool message from the far off clouds,
My soul is drooping 'neath its gathered dust—
Drop down thy starry dews and quench its thirst,
Oh Truth divine! and make me strong
To seek Thee evermore—and seek *alone !*"

The congregation in a motley stream
Had poured out past him with averted eyes
And left him as a harmless half-crazed man
A stranger and alone among the tombs.

The witness ages vanished from the stand,
But, by the throne of Him who judged the world
Calm stood the steadfast seeker of the Truth
As one whose utmost toil was lost in peace.

A DREAM ANTHEM.

PRIEST.

BELIEVE ye in the Lord of Hosts, the Ruler of the sky,
The universal Mother heart, the Lowliest and Most
   High?
Believe ye Him, the Soul of all, who wears eternal space,
And lives, the moving vital thought of each created
   place?

CONGREGATION.

Aye! Aye! believe we in the Lord! and worship from
   afar
The King upon his great white throne above the farthest
   star!
We build up temples to his name, which pierce the very
   sky,
And shout our praises loud and long that he may heed
   our cry.

PRIEST.

Believe ye in life's holy Truths, whate'er may be their
   name;
Tho' scorned amid earth's chase for wealth, for pleasure
   or for fame?
Believe ye in the soul of Love, which claims each living
   thing,
However low, disgraced, or mean, the source from which
   they spring?

Aye! we believe in lofty Truth! Truth is great and
  nobly born!
But bow we *not* to thing so mean as to be sport for
  scorn!
And we believe in Love divine, all conquering and sweet,
But waste it not on outcast ones in the prison and the
  street.

Well speak ye of twin Love and Truth! right nobly
  born are they!
The right hand and the left of Him, the king to whom
  ye pray!
Eternal as our Sovereign Lord—the Lord of Heaven's
  high host,
The outcast Love! the slighted Truth! God's Son and
  Holy Ghost!

Look not above the farthest star! God whispers in the
  air,
And instinct with his breathing life glows nature every
  where.
The time will come! The time will come, when on every
  stick and stone
The blindest eye can but behold the Eternal's living
  throne!

On all the doors, on all the walls, from the threshold to
  the caves,
On all the buds and bursting flowers, ripe fruits and
  trembling leaves,

And on all things living shall ye see, as written on a
 scroll,
In characters of light glow forth the universal soul!

Believe ye in the Lord of Hosts?
(CONGREGATION.) Aye! believe we as before!
(PRIEST.) Believe ye that all Truth is God?
(CONGREGATION.) Aye! and worship evermore!

ALL.

We accept Thee, God of Mercy! Love, and Truth, and
 Life art thou!
Accept us while we bow before Thee! To no other do
 we bow.

Near Smethport, in Pennsylvania, there is a great pile of conglomerate rocks, known by the name of the Devil's Den. During a pic-nic
at the place once, a gentleman who demurred at the popular mode of
devoting all grandeur to "the gentleman in black," proposed taking
the first initial of each lady's name then present, and coining a name
for the place. The name was Eel-c-a-ha-o-aa see, so suggestively
Indiany in sound, that the following commemorative poem grew out
of it ever so many years ago:—

PART FIRST.

NATURE in wayward mood had thrown
O'er yon mountain's top a giant stone ;
The river's waves no longer rushed—
The wild bird's warblings were hushed—
The woods grew dark with sickening fear
 Its heart-pulse faint and cold,
As downward on their wild career
 The broken fragments rolled.
The re in rough disorder piled,
O'er that mountain wide and wild ,
'Mid tangled laurels, dark and rude,
The rocks grew grey in solitude.
The loosened earth slid slowly down,
Leaving the hill-side bare and brown.
It left the mountain's hoary head,
And rested in the valley's bed ;

The river's waters sought in vain
To trace their pebbly track again.
Back to their fountains, dark and cold,
The imprisoned waters slowly rolled;
'Till upward 'gainst the opposing heap
    They wider, mightier, rose;
Then o'er its brink they wildly leap,
    Free from their dull repose.
The river's dried, deserted track
Welcomed the fresh, pure waters back.

High on the mountain's dusky brow,
Defying wintry storms and snow,
Three walls of solid stone uprose,
And o'er their massive, grim repose,
Rested a roof of one great stone,
With creeping evergreens o'ergrown.
By the low doorway on the east
Sat that lone mountain's hermit priest.
Near, thro' mossy crevice, crept
Waters where the lichens slept;
Drop by drop those waters fell
In a moss-enamelled well,
Near that grey old hermit's cell.

Across the lake, and on its brim,
In the forest's shadow dim,
A wigwam raised its lowly head
Close beside the water's bed,
And in that hut a warrior bold
In prosperous peace was growing old.
His sons were " swiftest in the race,"
Their bows were surest in the chase;

His daughters, with fond mothers' pride,
Their children's tottering footsteps guide,
Save one—the flower of vale or hill,
Who watched, and loved, and cheered him still.
Evening was rosy in the west,
And tipped with gold each mountain's crest,
When a tall form, as oft before,
Darkened that lowly wigwam door;
Strong was his soul and firm his tread,
Ere the low doorway bowed his head ;—
He spoke; Nayugch could not brook
The lightning of the chieftain's look.

" Old Eagle of the pine clad hills !
   A day of blood is breaking !
Sleep no more by purling rills,
   Thy warriors are waking.
Pale children of the rising day
Come like wolves upon their prey ;
Like wolves upon the wild deer's track !
Like panthers we will send them back !
To-morrow is our council held."
Then forth he hied—the war-whoop yelled—
And to some other brave's abode
The Cougar of the mountain strode.

The council met, then from the earth
The red war-hatchet sprang to birth;
The war-pipe's smoke 'tween the old oak limbs
Disturbed the wood-wren's matin hymns ;
And then arose to the peaceful skies
The smoke of the white dog sacrifice,

And to that sacrificial feast
Came Eel-e-a-ha-o-aa-see's priest,
From the lonely-mountain side,
Where none but he might dare abide,
Where naught polluting e'er might dwell,
From the moss-grown hermit's cell,
Where he his sacred treasure kept,
Guarding while he walked or slept,
That treasure that he deemed divine,
The sack of holy medicine;
Like the seraph-guarded ark,
　　Of which Scripture's pages tell;
Like a strayed and stranger spark,
　　From the fires of Israel!

'Twas over!　Then from south and north,
From east and west went warriors forth;
Armed with war-club, spear, and bow,
　　With tomahawk and knife;
Strong hands were there to deal each blow!
　　Strong hearts for blood and strife!
Then arose the war-whoop's fearful yell,
Wide over plain, and hill, and dell,
And echo came back from hill and glen,
Like the yell of demons instead of men;
And echo caught up the hideous cry,
And bore it aloft toward the burning sky.
Then silence o'er the valley crept,
As if all things living slept.
The wild birds' morning songs were o'er,
The hum of man was heard no more,—
Not a breath of wind there stirred,

Not the faintest sound was heard,
Save where the lake leaped from its thrall,
Dashed the noisy waterfall;
But the leaves its babbling drowned
Into a sadder, softer sound.
The smoky air wrapped every hill,
And seemed to hush its waters still;
But the silence was too deep,
Too unnatural for sleep.

In Eel-e-a-ha-o-aa-see's cell,
The priest was chanting o'er his spell,
While watching, more in awe than fear,
Stood the father of the youthful Deer,
While she, Nayugch, stood afar,
And prayed to the God of peace and war,
To send her Father safely back
From the war-path's dangerous track.
Then in her heart a stifled prayer,
That to breathe she did not dare,
For the Cougar that stood gazing on,
The Hermit and his myrmidon.

The Hermit watched his magic fire,
Whose blue flame flickered pale and dire;
As he muttered his spells in a tongue unknown
To a fiercer blaze was his watch-fire blown;
Quickly the red flame leaped on high,
With a glory that paled the burning sky,
And eagerly seizing a pine tree's stem,
It crowned its cone with a diadem;
With its wreaths of smoke and its tongues of flame,

A terrific torch that tree became.
Then sudden the yell of the Hermit rang,
Till the echoing hills caught up the clang—
Then sunk his voice to a muttering tone—
Then chanted as if to himself alone.

" Not till yon lake shall cease to spread,
Over the quiet valley's bed,
Not till the weeds that in it stand,
Flourish upon the naked land—
Not till its barrier is strewn,
Where Nonandah's limpid waters moan,
Not till yon lake deserts the glen,
Shall we yield to a race of paler men—
When the Lake of the Forest no more shall be,
Our tribe shall die like the foam of the sea.!"

He ceased his low, complaining wail,
The warriors sought the foemen's trail—
Nayugeh sought with wondering gaze,
The pine tree torch's brilliant blaze,
Which stood aloft like a beacon light,
Lighting the shades of coming night,—

" Why follows the Deer on the Cougar's track?
Will the Wild Doe welcome the Panther back?"
Nayugeh turned with a startled sigh
To meet the dark inquiring eye
Of a sister beloved who was standing nigh.
" Come, sister, my lonely wigwam share—
'Tis gloomy unless the loved are there,
The Eagle has flown toward the morning sky,

There are none to comfort or keep thee nigh,
But we'll gather herbs from the solemn wood,
And draw the fish from the silver flood,
And watch and wait till our warriors come
Together to welcome the wearied home."

PART SECOND.

"I came, O Wild Doe of the hills!
Back to my native rocks and rills,
With my life blood ebbing slow away,
From a wound whose bleeding I cannot stay.
Ye cannot follow on our track,
And I may never more come back;
Where canst thou flee in the hour of wrath,
When the Eagle has fallen in war's red path,
When the Cougar is far from Nayugeh's call,
Will the child of the forest die in thrall?"

Nayugeh had watched his kindling eye—
Her bosom was burning to make reply;
But a daughter's love and a maiden's fears
Burst forth in a passionate gush of tears;
From her sobbing lips no answer came,
Save a murmuring of her father's name.

"Cold on the far off plain of death,
Sighed forth thy father's dying breath;
And I alone am left to tell,
Where the Eagle of the mountains fell.
No pale face bore his scalp away,
He lies no colder there than they."

"Thou hast avenged him then!" she said,
Raising her lone and sorrowing head,
"But hast come alone from that dreadful fray?
My Warrior brothers, where are they?"

"Cold on the battle field they lie!"
Was the mountain Cougar's sad reply,
"Our shattered tribe are gathering,
Weak like the flow of a sun-dried spring;
But the pale men came like a river's tide,
When the snow melts off the brown hill side;
Whither, oh! Doe of the forest dark!
Wilt guide thy canoe of the birchen bark?
Where, oh! maiden mild and meek!
Hide where the pale men will not seek,
For their hounds can follow thy footsteps well?"
Nayugeh murmured, "I cannot tell!"

"Follow me, Nayugeh, in this mountain path,
What though the storm God growl in wrath?
Is the eyrie rocked eaglet of tempests afraid!"
"No!" said the voice of the following maid.

On, dark rolled the river, its wild rising flood,
Fierce howled the storm through the loud wailing
    wood,
Yet up through the shrieking tempest's wrath,
They follow that tree strewn mountain path,
Up, past the Hermit's empty cell,
Up, where the trees wild crashing fell—
Up, where each grim rock raised its head,
Where Eel-e-a-ha-o-aa-see spread

Its platform dark of giant stones,
Above the wrung trees' crashing groans,
Here the Mountain Cougar climbed at last,
And paused—his clambering was past,
At length Nayugeh near him drew,
Her weary march was ended too.

A ragged aisle the wind had made
Down before them to the glade.
The pent lake's waters rose up still,
Chafing the foot of the rocky hill.
Ah ! never before since those cabins stood,
In the shadowy marge of the wide-spread wood,
Had risen so high that river's flood—
When the mountains shook and the valleys groan,
With an echoing crash in thunder tone—
The barrier burst !   The Lake was gone !—
And the cabins that stood on the outlet's shore,
Were lost in the waves and seen no more.

" We are the last !" the Cougar said,
" The lake is gone—our tribe is dead—
Ere night shall darken o'er the sky,
The Cougar of the Hills must die,
And one lone Doe in the pale man's path,
Is all that is left to stem his wrath—"

" Oh better, far better to die with thee !"
Responded the wild Doe earnestly.
How glow'd o'er the face of the dying chief,
The light of a smile as bright as brief !
Then answered he with a deep drawn sigh,

" I brought thee here with me to die!
O! deeply these rifted rocks between,
With a feathery fern and a laurel screen,
To whisper with winds that are floating by,
'Twere sweet for the last of the tribe to lie—
'Twere sweet for the Panther and Doe to die!"

The moss grown rocks the notes prolong,
As they sang together their funeral song.

Howl! tempest in the forest, howl!
    One tribe no more shall heed or hear!
Above them shall the wild wolf prowl,
    And undisturbed pursue the deer.

Weak are the hands once strong in battle,—
    Cold are the hearts once warming our home,—
The bones of our braves the foxes shall rattle,
    Over each heart's deserted stone.

We come to Thee, great ruling Spirit!
    To thy happiest hunting ground—
The land that the good and the brave inherit,
    That the pale face has not found!

They ceased, the Cougar's failing arm,
    Was round the form he loved the best,
He seemed to shelter her from harm—
    He looked as if he but caressed.
Then kneeling on the giddy brink,
    He sheathed his knife within her heart—
Then in his own. The mosses drink
    The blood of those who would not part.

O! deeply those rifted rocks between,
With a feathery fern and a laurel screen,
To whisper with winds that are floating by,
The last of the tribe of the Eagle lie.
The Lake of the Forest no more shall be,
And its tribe are gone like the foam of the sea.

PART I. THE PRELUDE.

Orthodox according to Romances; Apocryphal according to Fact.

NEAR a "dark rolling river" by "willows o'erhung,"
  Stood a "lowly white cottage" with shutters of
    green,
Where the creeping vines round the windows clung,
And the "gnarled old oak" its shadow flung,
  A broad armed and beautiful screen;
Round one room the flowers were growing
  "With a mute caress,"
As tho' thro' shadowy foliage showing
  "The inmate's loveliness."
For "lovely as the morning" smiled
That "sweet and lovely" "forest child."
Her eyes were "liquid hazel," beaming
  'Neath the "dark fringe of each lid,"
Her "alabaster neck" was gleaming,
  Half by its "curling drapery hid."
Her beauty might bewitch the sight
Of any frigid anchorite;
  But the "soul that beamed within"
  Was something deeper than the skin!

Young Oscar from the mill one day,
Chanced to be wandering by that way,
When to milk the cows, thro' the river's slime
Waded the barefooted Angeline.
They met beneath the spreading tree,
And "their first glance" "sealed their destiny!"
While seated on the milking stool,
Beneath the willow's shade so cool,
The maiden sang a song more sweet
Than songs which summer evening greet.
A joyous thrill through each nerve sprang
As the music tone through his young heart rang—
Full many a glance she sidelong cast,
Ere those hours on golden wings had passed.
His "manly form" and comely face,
He bore with manhood's budding grace;
And his voice, tho' low, was deep and full,
As he sang with the maid on the milking stool.

He carried the pail, o'er-topped with foam,
To Angeline's vine-covered bright "happy home,"
Then through that soft and star-lit sabbath eve
    He sat on the porch by young Angeline's side;
Bright visions of hope together they weave,
    Ere the "launch on life's dark fathomless tide."
They part when the waning moon rose bright,
And shed o'er earth its "silvery light"—
If you wish to know what vows they made,
What deeds they did, and what says they said,
You must ask of somebody wise in such lore,
For I wasn't there, and can tell no more,
Save that ever when seven days wheeled their flight,

And bro't again the Sabbath night,
Did Oscar sit by that cottage fire,
And list to a tale from the grey-haired sire;
And tho' long and tedious the tale became,
To Oscar's ears it was still the same;
For no heed could he give to the tale of strife,
He could only think of his future wife.
Tho' mute and attentive he seemed to be,
His thoughts were working busily,
As he built a castle of azure air,
In which to dwell with his chosen fair.
Thus time flew by, as he always will,
Let us wish e'er so much to make him stand still,
And Oscar so long had worked in the mill,
    That his earnings would buy him a snug little farm;
So away to his lot in the woods went he
To fell and to burn each tall forest tree,
    And make him a cabin tight and warm.
Thought he, " when 'tis finished, and snug, and neat,
I'll throw myself at Angeline's feet,
    And tell her to name the day;
Then hither we'll hie from the world away,
And spend in labor the hours gay,
    Till eve brings a season of quiet rest;
    And then together in our nice little nest,
We'll sing some ballad or 'olden lay,'
    And be 'purely and perfectly blest.' "

PART II.

*The Afterclap ignored by romances—being the main
body of life's matter-of-fact.*

'Twas done—the hymenial knot was tied—
The maid of sixteen was a bride ;
The groom was of a riper age,
For twenty years had made him sage ;
That *sagesse* made him build a mill
Upon his winding mountain rill ;
Hard by he reared his humble cot,
Nor envies kings their higher lot.
Thither his slow ox-team he drives,
　　Dragging behind a groaning cart,
Which shrieked as if a cat's nine lives
　　Were in it, struggling to depart.
No wonder ; cart of mortal make
Could not endure it—it must break.
Just as it jolted o'er a stone
　　High swelling in the road,
The cart gave one prodigious groan,
　　And fell splash in the mud !
The axle broke, what could he do,
Unless he sunk in the mud-hole too ?
Despair seized on him for a time,
But loosed his hold as Angeline
Proposed the furniture to save
From sinking in a miry grave.
He seized the tho't—with all his might
He threw the goods both left and right,

Resolved to resurrect the cart,
 He made an axle-tree of wood,
 Which, if it wasn't very good,
Still served to cheer his heart,
And bear his replaced chattels on,
" Over root and mossy stone."

Tho' the honeymoon was over,
Oscar Rose was still a lover,
And felt a lover's full vexation
Because it rained " like all creation,"
And March winds blew their fiercest chime,
To welcome home his Angeline.
" Ah, love !" he cried, " what shall we do ?
The roof leaks streams and puddles too,
But here's a place quite dry for you."
" Oh, well ;" she said, " I'll go to work,
And cook potatoes, eggs, and pork,
 If you'll set up the stove—"
" Yes, yes !" and then to work he went,
 While rain his garments soak ;
But part of the stove was badly bent,
 And part was fully broke ;
But they fixed it up, and made it do,
And Angeline cooked a smoky stew,
(For the cracked stove leaked both smoke and ashes,
 And the wind in fitful gusts
The rain through every chink hole dashes,
 And blew in pecks of moss and dust.)
They ate it (not the *dust*, but stew),
And went to work with zeal anew.
Oscar o'erhead stopped out the sky,

The cracks were stopped—the floor mopped dry—
And then fatigued beyond all measure,
They went to sleep and snored with pleasure.

Next morn the sun rose clear and bright,
They eat their meal with appetite,
And Oscar hastened back to town,
 To fetch another load ;
This time he didn't quite break down,
 Nor upset in the road.
So everything was "fixed" all right
Before there closed another night ;
So they were settled in a trice
Snug as a nest of tiny mice.

Oscar's father died, and his stepmother came,
With her mother who was blind, and deaf, and lame,
 To live with him and his deary—
Tho' deaf, not dumb, was Grandame Hill,
For her tongue ran on, like the cork leg still,
 Tho' all ears with din were weary ;
Then she was so cross she couldn't be endured,
Excepting because she couldn't be cured.
 The stepdame was one vast interrogation—
Minding all business that wasn't her own—
She would whine all the time to make her griefs known,
 And scold with a voice like the Bull of Bashan ;
Then talk of her pious faith and labor,
And then, next minute, slander her neighbor.
Angeline had six "sweet little dears,"
That oft got boxed on their "sweet little" ears,
By the stepdame's grandmotherly hand,

Because in the way they happened to stand,
Or could not reply to some interrogation
That she made in her tours of investigation.

No secret cell did the house afford
Where Angeline could hide a secret hoard,
   Or where aught could secret be;
For every drawer, and trunk, and chest,
Was an object of curious interest,
   The stepdame all must see ;
If opposed she'd sigh as if wounded to death,
And say with a kind of sobbing breath,
" Ah, why am I doomed on earth to live,
And no respect from my child receive ?"
Then she would cry and sulk for a week,
And her malice dire on the children wreak.
Then she'd a daughter, a squint-eyed girl,
   Who'd married, in spite of her friends,
An ugly, piratical looking churl,
   Who, to make most ample amends
For all his numerous peccadillos,
   And to appease a fit of rage,
   Took an anonymous pilgrimage
Across the foaming Erie's billows,
And ne'er returned to Sylvia more ;
But left to heal her widowed heart,
That his desertion might make sore,
   A small edition of himself,
   A little, silly, roaring elf,
That Sylvia's switch oft caused to smart.
Her husband's debts his goods consume,
So Sylvia had no house or home ;

So trusting unto Providence,
And her step-brother's benevolence,
She took herself and darling boy,
His bounteous mansion to enjoy.

If Sylvia's baby mightn't run over
    Every child of Angeline's,
She'd tell Dame Hill, and her own cross mother,
    And then would follow a chorus of whines.
If Oscar and Angeline ever went out,
    Mrs. Rose and Sylvia 'd pursue them—
"Why, children! what are you talking about?"
Mrs. Rose would say, and begin to pout,
    "I wish the world only knew them!
They treat me as if I were only a stranger!
    Stop talking if I but come nigh!
I believe they'd grudge me hay in a manger!"
    And then she'd begin to cry.

Dame Hill would tell monstrous long stories,
    So loud that herself could hear,
About her good man's fights with the tories,
    Her husband, that "poor lost dear."
She had placed goods in Oscar's possession,
    Worth some thirty dollars and odd,
And she deemed it a horrid aggression
    If Oscar hung not on her nod.
"Ingrate! I brought him his wealth,
    Now he won't mind a word that I say!
Oh! if I could but have my health,
    I'd go with my money away!"

"And just see how poor Silvy is used!"
    Mrs. Rose then put in her word—
"I never saw girl so abused!
    Of such abuse I never have heard!
She helps Angy wash, and takes care of her child
(Just see what a heap on the table they've piled);
She takes care of the chambers, and waits upon you,
And all this she does without wages, too!
Poor girl! because she's unfortunate,
Such advantage as this of her misery take!
Oh! shame on the wretches who thus can doom
An orphan widow to poverty's gloom!
Make use of her labor, and when 'tis done,
Give her only support for herself and son!"

"Yes, shameless indeed!" cried Grandame Hill,
"Oscar has a farm, and house, and mill,
And money can raise when he wants, if he will—
    Why don't he reward her well?"
Dame Hill had heard what her daughter said,
For she spoke in a tone that might wake the dead,
    And shame St. Paul's church bell—
Then both the old "ladies" began to cry,
And wish that they might quickly die—
    Then scolded, sighed, and sobbed all at once—
Dame Hill must hear every word that was said,
Or else she'd take it in her obstinate head
    That they thought her a deaf old dunce;
So she was apprised of all that went on,
Tho' her sight, and hearing, and strength were gone!

There was a bachelor uncle—a drunken sinner—

Was too stingy to afford his own bread and dinner,
Half the time loafed at Oscar's good table—
Gave orders about managing farm and stable—
Taught the children to smoke, and drink, and chew,
And say with each breath the innocents drew
   Some profane or unseemly word;
Until the parents turned him out,
And he left with an injured air and pout ;
   And the next thing that they heard,
Was that the wretch had suddenly died,
And left his wealth to Frederic Hyde,
   Sylvia's idiot baby !
'Twould be twenty years before he could touch
The hoards that cost his uncle so much,
   Yet Sylvia now thought her a lady !

Oscar and Angeline lived in fear,
Lest all their words Dame Rose should hear ;
They dare not talk till she was asleep,
And then awake they couldn't keep,
'Till one Sabbath they strayed to a beechen grove,
To talk of the days of their early love.

"I had dreamed," said Oscar, " of a happy lot,
With friends surrounding our little cot,
   Ourselves doing good and no evil—
And we *do* do good—there are grandma and mother,
They scold enough to fright the devil,
And we bear it and let it pass over.
I thought when we married and moved here home,
That we would quietly live alone,
   Enjoying felicity pure ;

'Stead of that, what quiet or peace do we get?
Grandma's in one perpetual fret,
And mother, who sees, torments us more yet.
    What evils we have to endure!"
"Then mother scolds," began Angeline,
"If I dare to think that the house is mine—
If I don't do as she bids she begins to cry,
And say, 'Of course you know better than I;
I'm but an old fool you all despise!'"
And she pours out a torrent of sighs,
    And grumbles and scolds all the time.
Then she knocks round the children as if they were wood,
That she wanted to hurt if she possibly could,
And complains of Sylvia's hard lot—
I ventured to hint we'd build them a cot,
Where they in tranquil peace might rest,
Where the children would ne'er their quiet molest!"
"That's the thing!" cried Oscar, "The very plan!
I'll build the cottage as soon as I can,
    And be rid of this troublesome pest!"
"Stop! stop! not so fast!" cried Angeline;
"When I told her this she began to whine,
And vowed she knew full well before,
We wanted to drive them from the door!"

"Well then, let's endure it as long as we can,
For mortal life is but a span—
Sylvia may marry—the old woman die—
(I'm sure if they did I shouldn't cry)—
And then we might live in comfort and ease,
With our children around us in quiet and peace;
Were we rich we might furnish ourselves a room,

Secure from a witch that could ride a broom,
 And these step-dames' tongues defy !
But henceforth let none but a fool in his dotage,
Dream of comfort and peace with 'Love in a Cottage!'"

MEN lived in tents, and tended roaming herds,
　　Ere, sprung alike from earth and heaven arose
Twin brother spirits, that with majestic words
　　Beckoned a palace from the quarries close,
And, fashioned out of common clay, they chose
　　A puny mortal, and nicknamed him king.
A waste of splendor round him they dispose;
　　And other mortals came to worshipping
　　That mortal for his show and glittering.

And yet through human hands alone they wrought,
　　To dig out treasures from the darkling mine;
To sculpture monuments of pride and thought,
　　Or frame the lyre, or pour the song divine;
Or do great deeds the numbing hand of time
　　Would pass untouched when thrones had crumbled low;
And mingled with oblivion's wasting slime,
　　They loved alike to raise or overthrow,
　　To toil 'mid torrid sands or everlasting snow.

And they were loved and hated, praised and jeered;
　　Oft victims both of flattery and scorn;
Dreaded and courted, idolized and feared,
　　They dared the wrath of foe, and time, and storm.
Men blest and cursed the hour when they were born,
　　And yet earth blossomed and the low wind sighed;
They thawed no snow and chilled no sunshine warm,

And yet have men arisen, lived and died,
And scarcely knew when with the twain that there
was aught beside.

Ambition! Genius! How your names can flash
Electric fire across the sluggish soul;
As in the stagnant air loud thunders crash,
And shake the welkin with their sudden roll.
So oft they burst thro' custom's strong control,
And shake the spirit with their lofty tone;
And from equator to each distant pole
Earth yields them tribute from each circling zone,
And man has bowed, a willing slave before their glow-
ing throne.

But once when men had caught their burning flame,
And taught its light on loathsome scenes to glow,
Burned hamlet, city, palace, hut, and fane,
And their mad shouts rose up as if to show
How men could joy in utter human woe.
When priests had thrown their sacred garb around
Each hideous sin mankind can ever know,
When sweet humanity's soft voice was drowned
In the great war of warring hosts, and discord's
jarring sound.

Then Truth in sorrow veiled her radiant head,
And Falsehood reigned above a darkened world;
When pitying Mercy wept unnumbered dead,
From out fierce tyrants' bloody pathway hurled;
When up from human fuel slowly curled
The blackening smoke of persecution's rage,
The twain in sadness then their pinions furled,

For Hist'ry 'd written on her bloody page,
" Ambition lit War's wasting torch, and led his pilgrim-
    age."

And men arraigned him at their judgment bar;
    The great blind multitude, who only knew
That 'mid the clamor of each feudal jar,
    Or war of nations, or of robber crew,
Ambition's torch o'er all its red light threw,
    And loud, 'mid clarion's, and 'mid trumpet's bray,
His voice of thunder rolled and echoed through;
    They knew not that the light was stolen away
    From hallowed altars, and profaned amid the fray.

They knew not that that pealing tone
    Was sounding ever on thro' space and time;
But unto glowing, high-wrought souls alone,
    Pealed forth its anthems or its triumph chime.
But those who caught it often linked with crime
    The words of power that they caught from Heaven;
They charged to Him, the generous and sublime,
    The evil that man's crime alone had given.
    They banished him, and forth that glowing soul was
    driven.

His brother stood unnoticed in the throng,
    His dark eye dimmed with sorrow's scowling cloud
He loved the right, but felt the power of wrong,
    Saw it, and heard it, 'mid the surgings loud
Of that great monster, the wrong-headed crowd;
    Yet not by anger, nor by pride, nor fear,
Was Genius' spirit for a moment bowed;

Half-wept he one disdainful, pitying tear,
  Then with his brother took his flight half round the
  sphere.

A darkness settled on the blind old world,
  A mist of apathy and stagnant gloom
From dull, inactive slothfulness, upcurled,
  And mould and mildew grew on glory's tomb.
And science' buds were blighted ere their bloom,
  And art was banished 'mid forgotten things,
To mourn the glory of her by-gone noon ;
  And music snapt her sweet vibrating strings,
And poesy 'mid deepest shade furled up her shining
  wings.

But fast and far across the waters blue—
  The rolling billows of the ocean's surge—
The twain in silence yet unwearied flew,
  'Till they had touched its forest-tasselled verge.
No more their flight so constantly they urge,
  But paused, and glancing where they late passed
    o'er,
Saw from the flood a pall-like mist emerge,
  And float off darkly towards that distant shore
Whence they had come. They sighed, and turned to
  flight once more.

Fate drove the exile far across the land,
  Deep to the bosom of a giant rock,
And chained him down with stern despotic hand,
  Where his cold dungeon evermore would mock

7

His restless spirit, while the tempest's shock
  And zephyr's murmur far above his cell
Made not a sound to pierce the solid block,
  Where strong Ambition had been doomed to dwell,
  Where Genius followed him, self-exiled when he fell.

And they were left alone, and darkness stood
  Stiff, palpable, and visible around,
Above—beneath—while all her monster brood
  Of hideous fancies throng the gloom profound.
How fared he then—that exile doomed and bound?
  The proud, aspiring, progress-spirit then?
Hope could not breathe one single cheering sound,
  And chill Despair came o'er his life again,
  Though oft repulsed in scorn—like all his faith in
    men.

Ne'er on his path had Hope refused to smile;
  Ne'er had he faltered or despaired before;
Thwarted and crushed, had lain in dust awhile;
  Then like a whirlwind on a tropic shore,
Burst he to life and energy once more.
  In life's rough discipline, in school or field,
One word he ne'er had conned or pondered o'er;
  Against one lesson had his heart been steeled,
  He could not, would not learn the bitter words—*to*
    yield.

But now an hour of dull and death-like dread
  Came o'er his soul—a with'ring agony,
Such as men feel who have no tears to shed,
  When they have drunk such drops of misery

As few can live to bear—he breathed no sigh;
  He spoke no word; not e'en a thought broke thro'
That stunning dread. He knew he could not die,
  And yet no hope for future years he drew.
  He had been conquered—this was all he felt or
  knew.

A voice whose silvery sweetness softly fell,
  Like the low ripples on a shell-strewn shore,
Or dying echo of a distant bell,
  Broke through his trance—his gush of passion o'er,
He started up—a spell those accents bore
  To fright despair. "Look up!" those words were all
That made Ambition like himself once more—
  He stood within a lofty lighted hall,   ·
  While round him rose a thousand pillars white and tall.

Bewildered—glad, and awed almost to fear,
  He stood one moment; bursting then aloft,
Rose his wild shout that echo loved to hear,
  Catching it up and uttering full oft,
The joy cry loud, till whispering low and soft
  The murmurs far in distant music die,
" I am not conquered! tho' exiled and scoffed
  By man's decree and blind old destiny,
  'Twas but a moment that I stooped enough to sigh."

He paused till echo rolled and died away,
  Like an imprisoned thunder sunk to sleep,
And stillness followed its tumultuous play,
  Heavy—profound—like death's abysmal deep,

Whose gates the voiceless shades for ever keep;
  Awe fell upon his spirit and he spoke,
Subdued and soft as summer zephyr's sweep—
    "Was that thy voice, my brother?" yet it broke
    The spell of silence, and a thousand whispers woke.

"My brother!" "brother!" "thine my brother!"
    "thine!"
Mingled in murmurs, wildering to hear,
Confused and strange as sounds the morning chime
  Of wild birds warbling their heart-stirring cheer
A flood of clashing music full and clear,
  Upon the wondering and repeating air,
Till the vibrations half beguile the ear,
    To think no music so surpassing rare,
    As those wild echo-glees that woodsmen only share.

But mingling with those waves of echo came,
  A voice he knew could not be all his own,
Familiar accents spoke the exile's name,
  With deep affection in its low-breathed tone:
He knew—he felt—he was not all alone—
  The proud exultings of his heart grew still,
A half-shed tear within his eyelids shone—
    A world was powerless to break his will,
    And yet 'one word could thus his stubborn spirit
      thrill.

"Now who is thwarted, Destiny or thee?
  Where is thy cell, of earth thy destined part?
Can bungling man inspired by golden fee,
  Carve such a palace from the mountain's heart?

Can their ideals thus to being start ?
  Their glowing thoughts congeal to solid stone,
Without the tardy aid of feeble art ?
  A city might lie dwarfed beneath this dome,
  That by my will I built for love of thee alone!

" O brother! with a heart of earnest love,
  And strong free faith in truth's unfailing power,
With will unflinching as the stars above,
  One well may balk earth's most exultant hour,
Of half its triumph. What tho' Fate may lower,
  And men obedient echo back her ban ?
The wrath of mortals, like a summer shower,
  Falls and is past ; and hate's most bitter plan,
  Dies with the failing life of poor, short-sighted man.

" Thou art a strong, and I a wayward one,
  Without thee, oft I ramble bootless where
Thy eagle eye and spirit-stirring tone,
  Would rouse up hosts thy energy to share ;   \
Thou from the desert, and the mountains bare,
  Would force out action by incessant toil,
While I, too oft in valleys rich and fair,
  Riot mid nature's most luxuriant spoil,
And leave unwrought the strength of that unbroken soil.

" But when with thee, for me the deserts bloom,
  I make a palace of a dungeon cell,
Despair's dark night with Hope's wild fires illume,
  And change doom's mutterings to the wavy swell
Of music witching as a fairy spell ;
  With me thy footsteps blaze with glowing light,
And like the chime of a cathedral bell,

Thy voice, o'er ocean surge and mountain height,
Peals forth in thunder tones thy words of might.

"Henceforth let us be one, a Dual One,
    That, whom thou lovest, him I too shall love—
We'll reap together what we both have strewn,
    And strew together wheresoe'er we rove;
But should I tarry in some myrtle grove,
    While far beyond thy prouder footsteps stray,
Then, whom I bless thy spirit shall not move,
    But he shall be like those red lights that play
    O'er northern nights—as aimless and as vague as
        they.

"Bird-like he'll tune his nature-prompted song,
    Nor seek to leave his native tangled shade,
No motive power shall urge his course along,
    By impulse started and by impulse stayed,
Prompted by feelings that he never weighed,
    One hour he'll sigh o'er some imagined ill,
And joys, like Autumn leaves, will dim and fade,
    And then as sudden, with a joyous thrill,
    Pleasure shall crown life's cup that all the graces
        fill.

"Unknown to me some mortal shouldst thou name,
    That soul shall feel Ambition's force alone—
Will toil from land to land—from main to main,
    To carve his name on rocks of every zone;
Each desert rock to him shall seem a throne,
    Seen thro' hope's mirage, ever drawing near,
His barren path shall ne'er be overgrown,

With bloom I strew as I have strewn it here!
He shall be hard and cold and held in awe and fear.

" But he to whom we both our blessings give,
    Shall mow the forests like the blooming grass,
Or plough the mountains or subdue the wave,
    Or far aloft the wilds of æther pass,
Or touch the pulses of the human mass,
    And count its heart throes and find out the word
That' rules like magic o'er the populace vast—
    The word of power stronger than the sword,
    And where he listeth he shall rule the people as their
        lord!"

How the Dark Ages slowly rolled away,
    And Destiny recalled the exiled pair,
How new life struggled with the old decay,
    And new hope wrestled with the old despair,
Is it not writ in Hist'ry's pages fair?
    And they who led the exodus from night,
Who brought up buried truths to upper air,
    For blindfold science, who found out the light,
    Were they not gifted of the twain—the Strong soul
        and the Bright?

THE eyes of men are failing with looking up so long,
For fleetness to outrace the swift, and strength to fight
  the strong;
And their faith is full of doubting, when God's lightnings
  seem in vain,
To melt the ice from human hearts, or rive the bond-
  man's chain.
And the lip hath learned to murmur at the law ill
  understood,
Which sends the sun and rain alike on the evil and the
  good;   .
And the heart grows sick and weary that the seed so
  freely sown,
So often falls on barren sand, and cold unyielding stone;
That words return so dull and void, that went forth
  strong and full
Of truth's most earnest prophecies against oppression's
  rule,
And when he, like the seer of old, would call down scath
  and fire,
Heaven's blue serene but seems to mock his soul's impa-
  tient ire.

He sees a nation's garments grown, by threat and lash-
  paid toil;
He hears a murdered brother's blood cry ceaseless from
  the soil;

He sees no forest deep enough in all our wide-spread
    land,
To shield the crimeless fugitive from the oppressor's
    hand.
A stranger rests within thy gates—a weary one is he—
What boots his name, or hue, or race? What matters
    it to thee?
Ahungered, cold, athirst, he comes—thy bounty gushes
    free;
A Saviour's tones approving say, " Thou doest it to me."
But hark! is that a bloodhound's bay? Why comes its
    howling here?
Why turns the stranger's tranquil brow aghast with
    sudden fear?
O! woe for him, that hunted one! thou canst not
    give him rest;
Thy household altar cannot shield that "welcomed
    stranger guest;"
The Marshal and his minions full armed are on his track,
To his loathsome house of bondage to bear God's image
    back.
No homestead walls, no fireside hearths, are sacred from
    the hands
Of human vampyres such as these, who scourge our
    slave-curst land.

What wonder that men's souls grow sick at all this woe
    and wrong?
What wonder that their faith is weak, when Evil seems
    so strong?
She boasts her strength with voice of pride, and down
    before her fall

The leaders they had watched and hoped would break
her iron thrall.

Then trust not to such wandering stars, to *each* a soul
is given;

Each has his own peculiar work to do for earth and
heaven.

We read a fallen leader drew a third of Heaven's bright
host

Down to that grim and black abyss, where all were
merged and lost.

Then follow not blind, erring guides, when GOD can
lead us all;

We owe allegiance to none else, we need no other's
call.

The arm of flesh is faint and weak, and if the spirit fail,

O! when in all this outraged world will truth and peace
prevail?

When the half-wrecked ship is drifting upon the stormy
sea,

The sailor has no time to pause and wail despairingly.

Storm-worn and dripping with the brine of many a bil-
low's crest,

The weary battler with the waves can find no time to
rest.

And now this whelming tide of wrong the bark of truth
has tossed,

Till hope's dim beacon, 'mid its wrath, seems well-nigh
drowned and lost;

Yet all the more with earnest grasp hold fast the driving
wheel,

And steer amid the breaking surf our good ship's stubborn keel.

The weary must not heed their toil, nor weak ones
count their fears ; .
The mourner must forget his grief—there is no time for
tears ;
The night watch must not miss our work, or when this
driving storm
Shall break before the blazing wheels that bring the
coming morn,
We shall not see the riven clouds fall dead and prone
apart,
And from their very blackest midst the genial sunlight
start.
Take courage, weary toiler ! Heaven whispers earnest
cheer;
For ever when we least expect, the light and help draw
near,
For we know that GOD is with us—that for the *man* he
gave,
He will not take from master's hands a chattel soul—a
slave.
Ah, spoilers ! tremble when he calls, for that manhood
robbed away ;
For the host of rights and duties you are snatching from
your prey ;
Oh ! soldiers, on truth's battle-field, with your arms of
love and light !
I charge ye, faint not—GOD has pledged the victory to
the right.

Like to a lake the stream before me lieth,
  Between a rocky and a wooded shore,
Cradling the many tints where daylight dieth,
  Repeating each expiring glory o'er.

And there the forest shadows shake and shimmer,
  In every ripple by the breezes curled,
All shapes are mingling in one common glimmer,
  Within that mirror's strange inverted world.

A white sail, like a sea-bird o'er it glideth,
  And floats behind the island's twilight grey
Where creeps a pale mist slowly up and hideth
  Whatever lieth in its milky way.

The blue Itasca would not know her daughter,
  So soiled with travel and so overgrown,
Who spreads yon rolling sea of turbid water,
  A thousand leagues out toward the burning zone.

From out the caverned bluff the night bird calleth,
  And from the quarry comes an answering cry,
The flitting double of the night hawk falleth
  Down where the other shivering shadows lie.

And one white star on night's cool forehead glistens,
  And glistens upward from the waves as well,

And with hushed breath my very spirit listens
  To some sweet music's far-off, dying swell.

I almost wish that I could do my sleeping
  With yonder wild birds on the river's breast,
And with the stars their ceaseless vigil keeping,
  Be like an infant once more rocked to rest.

SACRAMENT.

Up by the old road on the hill,
  Now with the creeping grass o'ergrown,
Near where the faintly springing rill
  Is oozing o'er the mossy stone—
Hard by the grouse's deep retreat,
  Through all this soft autumnal haze,
Wait for me at the old time seat,   .
  Dear Love of by-gone days!

The world is flushed with ceaseless change,
  Its brimming joy cup running o'er,
But weary of the new and strange,
  I long for our old haunts once more.
I long to tread each dear old hill,
  Beneath its woods of red and gold,
And 'mid their riches grand and still,
  Be soul-baptized within the Old.

Cease shivering, trembling Aspen tree—
  I would not have thy rustling heard!
Murmur not now, thou Pine wood sea!
  Sigh not, soft Wind! chant not, sweet Bird!
Lay thy dear hand in mine, my Own,
  That I may feel thy heart throbs near,
And take from God, with me alone,
  This Sacrament of Silence here.

YE may harness the lightning till trained like a steed,
It will carry your thoughts with its limitless speed,
Ye may yoke the fierce whirlwind till bowed to your
    will,
It will grind like the ox you have broke to your mill ;
Ye may tame the wild cataract's flood till it feels,
Like a felon condemned at your factory wheels ;
But there stay your strong hand, nor dare lengthen
    your chain,
E'er to harness a *soul* to your engines for gain.

Ye may desecrate Nature, and haughtily tread
On the wrecks of its beauty, disfigured and dead,
But 'twere better for you that ne'er from the sod
Ye had started to life, at the mandate of God,
If ye dare to subdue to your power the will
Of a soul, which, tho' crushed and distorted, is still
In the image of Him, who hath, equal and free,
Made that spirit, proud atoms of frailty, with ye !

We can toil for a purpose, and cling unto life,
Thro' its storms and its turmoil, temptations and strife,
While the purpose is high, and the motive is pure,
Few indeed are the trials we cannot endure.
But go—put your curb on another's free will,
Keep us back from our aim, yoke our souls in your mill,
Make our poverty something too bitter to bear,
Ye will see then how much a high purpose will dare.

We can sleep upon straw on the cold garret floor,
We can toil on the crusts Dives casts from the door,
We can shiver half clad by the unlighted hearth,
Tho' we quail at the sound of the northern wind's mirth.
We can bear it and smile if the heart food is there,
To urge on the free spirit to do and to dare;
Aye! can laugh at privation, and hunger, and cold,
And thro' scorn, tho' in rags, be strong-hearted and bold,
For we know that the wealth of Peru cannot buy
Our ambition's proud hope—or a home in the sky;
And each slight that we feel, and each sneer that we
    meet,
Adds fresh fire to our hearts, and gives wings to our feet;
Every force that opposed, when o'ercome makes us
    strong,
Gives us courage to battle with famine and wrong,
But dare bar up the path to our purpose, and see
If the poor in their might are not stronger than ye!

A GOLDEN cloud with silvery traces,
The *future*, floated on before,
Its border smiled with angel faces,
A double rainbow spanned it o'er.

The sunlight thro' its wingèd edges,
Shed a dreamy, mystic calm,
As o'er the mountain's serried ridges,
Unscarred by peak or crag it swam.

O'er my childhood trailed its shadow,
As unchildlike sad, I lay,
Beneath the old tree in the meadow,
Listening to the water's play.

And time's wooing winds were winning,
All my long days thitherward,
Unthought-of stretched life's path of sinning,
Pain-enhedged and fire-scarred—

The future gathered dark before me,
One grim cloud, streaked with sulph'rous dun;
It came to meet, it shadowed o'er me,
And life's battle seemed begun!

" O my dreaming!" cried my spirit,
" Is human life a storm like this?
Must I from childhood's gloom inherit,
Maturer grief for hoped-for bliss?"

"O! thou golden-clouded future!
   Angel-winged and rainbow-spanned!
Didst thou herald woe and torture,
   A mocking mirage 'mid life's sand?"

But that scathing future came not,
   Where fell its shadow, fierce and dread,
And my youth but shared the same lot,
   That my weary childhood had.

And my spirit felt such yearning,
   For a wider path to tread,
Its long task of patience learning,
   While it knew not where it led.

And then the future, like a morning
   Blank with fog, before me lay,
'Till my searching soul took warning,
   And turned its scanning to to-day.

Lo! my crampèd path expanded!
   Roses flushed its hedge of thorns!
The free air my soul demanded,
   Blew fresh with breath of summer morns.

Then my soul looked round in wonder;
   " Whence," it cried, " this brightened way?
Was this the promise of the thunder
   And the clouds of yesterday?"

" Have my cheerless footsteps led me,
   Footsore up the mount of toil,
Where no friendly aiding sped me,
   To tread, at last, enchanted soil?"

The cloudlet of my childhood's vision,
  Around me spreads its hazy gold,
While onward, seeking realms elysian,
  The angel hosts their wings unfold.

How their great white pinions beckon,
  As on o'er gulf and crag they go!
Bridging chasms, thunder-stricken,
  With my child-dream's promise bow.

Then farewell, Hope! and farewell, fearing!
  Farewell, sighs for yesterday!
Since angel guards of faith and cheering
  Make life rich enough to-day!

" I LOVE thee !" the Apostle said,
Yet, ere another sun had shed
Its flood of light on tower and fane,
That friend denied the loved one's name,
And one more false and treacherous sold,
That priceless life for counted gold ;
Yet, who more loving seemed to be,
Ere that dark hour of wrath, than he ?

And yet the one they crucified—
The one his loving friend denied—
Was kind and gentle and more true
Than other friend earth ever knew,
Yet he found friends whose love grew cold,
Friends who denied him—friends who sold—
Friends who were never friends indeed,
And left him in his utmost need.

If false ones smote that gentle one,
So kind to all and harsh to none,
What erring child of earth may claim
A friendship deeper than a name ?
Tho' all may *seem* to love thee well,
Who, for the coming hour, can tell
Which of the friends who love in this
Will not betray him with a kiss ?
Who, ere life's changing sands are run,
'Mid all his friends is sure of one ?
Who, ere life's journey hath an end,
Will dare to say, " I have a friend ?"

I FELT the beating pulses of the cool and trembling sea,
    Thrill 'neath the silent touching of my earnest hand,
And the long bright ripples ran in meeting me,
    And leaped in laughter on the shell-strewn sand,
And my soul gushed up and over, as at clasp of friendly
    hand.

The sea-weeds rooted close, and clinging to some old
    and wave-worn shell,
    Cast their green and dripping tresses underneath my
      careless feet,
And the fairy foam-wreaths mounting every long and
    wavy swell,
    Tossed their white plumes on the air, and rushing
      glad and fleet
Dissolved in rainbows on the waves that murmured at
    my feet.

And the old and mythic dreamings of strange mystery
    and might
    That whispered their enchanting spells to my early
      childhood's ear,
Came flashing o'er my spirit's gloom, like broken gleams
    of light,
    Leaping from cloud-thrones drifting wide in the far
      off upper deep,
And then as sudden fading back to darkness and to sleep.

Then the soul within me, harness worked and labor
 tried,
  Arose and shook its shackles from each bondage
 wearied limb,
New strength seemed waking in me, new fervor and
 new pride,
  The new glory dawning on me made all earth-born
 glory dim,
And life transfigured stood before me, true of heart and
 free of limb!

Then life's battle seemed a conflict, not of pain, and toil,
 and woe,
  But more a war of wind and wave, of tempest and of
 sea!
And a stormy love of combat, in my veins began to glow,
  And heave my heart in great pulsations, in the joy of
 being free!
O! my soul grew brave and stronger from the teachings of the sea!

You ask me if I ever loved, and I most freely tell,
I *have* loved long and faithfully, loved earnestly and
  well,
Loved all things good and beautiful with love like wor-
  ship given,
Because I could not lock within the richest boon of
  Heaven:
Bind up the wind in some dark cave, and chain the
  restless sea,
Then prison in the human heart its springs of sympathy!
How can you ask of one like me, who on the earth so
  long
Has journeyed on life's pilgrimage, with all its changing
  throng?
O! I have loved, and there are none in this dark world
  of care,
Who in my heart's great sympathies have never held a
  share.
I've loved the tender and the cold, the worthless and
  the true,
Within my heart a bud of love for each thing human
  grew,
All things that breathe upon the earth, and e'en the
  very air,
The guiltless and the beautiful I have loved everywhere,
And yet in all this realm of love my heart has been a
  throne,

And he that sat thereon has ruled my spirit-land alone,
And obedient to my heart's enthroned, as to a god's
behest,
I've loved the world, the whole wide world, but my
own *will* the best.

How much is pride, that humble seems!
    How much is false, truth's guise that wears,
How patronizing kindness leans
    Its crushing weight on him who bears
The hateful mockery, as the saint
Bears fire and stake, without complaint.

'Tis hard in gratitude to bow
    And teach the stubborn lip to lie,
When the heart's writhing pride must glow,
    Insulted, in the cheek and eye,
Yet utter *thanks*, when it has borne
Man's stupid pity—worse than scorn!

It's not enough the struggling soul,
    Debarred from paths it fain would tread,
Must bow to fortune's stern control,
    And barter life for bitter bread—
Bitter with scorn's cold wormwood dew,
But must it bear man's pity too?

How strangely things are mixed and blended,
  Within the chaos of the brain!
Things unbegun with things long ended—
  Some of joy and some of pain.

Things as unlike as things well may be,
  Together through the soul's obscure,
Half float and sway in drifts unsteady,
  Like snow-wreaths on a wind-swept moor.

Just now a friend I made but newly,
  An old man, meek and quiet, came
Across my thoughts, which, all unruly,
  Have called him by another's name.

And oft of late this name he beareth,
  Within my spirit's unknown land,
Though ever his own form he weareth:
  What link between them made this band?

My first friend's eye was like the eagle,
  His frame with youth's strong sinews strung,
His voice, like call of silvery bugle,
  Around its strong-willed message flung.

A fireside look, and voice, and tread,
  My new friend hath, so sweetly human,
I turn and look at his snowy beard,
  And wonder he is not a woman!

Why should that name come thus, unbidden,
  To call on one so different far ?
Unlike as caves from sunshine hidden,
  And golden-blossomed prairies are.

They never met nor uttered greeting,
  Never heard each other's name—
Why in my thoughts do they keep meeting,
  As though they somehow were the same ?

LIKE the ripple of bright wavelets,
  On a beach of soft sea-sand ;
Like the flutter of the leaflets,
  In a wide-spread forest land ;

Like the footsteps of the rain-drops,
  In their dance upon the roof;
Or the ringing elfin echo,
  Of a fairy charger's hoof;

Like the hushed hive's low humming,
  When night's solemn rest has come,
Are the whisperings of our spirits,
  When we seek to be alone.

We listen to their murmur,
  Till their pleasant rustling seems,
As full-voiced, deep, and real,
  As the songs we hear in dreams.

The unreal's changing shadows
  With the real's substance blend,
Till forgotten lies life's riddle,
  And its fast-approaching end.

For the mists of death's dark valley,
  Rainbow arches bright o'erspan,
And beyond, in boundless sunshine,
  We behold the path of man !

Then what matter for the darkness,
   Closed within our prison bars,
When we know, that past its portals,
   All broad space is bright with stars!

When we know a whole world's shadow
   On the wilds of æther cast,
Down before heaven's watch-light dwindles
   To viewless point at last!

And at last when life emerges,
   With the faint breath from our lips,
And its glimmering light is hidden
   By grim death's cold, dread eclipse—

Shall that darkness break the fiat,
   By the universe obeyed,
And thus be, 'mid life, the only
   Eternity of shade?

" Nay !" these thousand voices answer,
   From the earth and upper air;
From the inmost restless spirit,
   Outspeaking everywhere.

Death is but the gateway, closing
   'Tween the old life and the new;
Have ye never seen it open,
   When a passing soul went through?

Though sometimes the darkness lieth
   Dim beyond the outer wall,
And no star-beam's brightness pierceth
   Through that heavy midnight pall—

And we sigh for the soul unlighted,
  Going down that lonely way;
For our eyes are unanointed,
  To behold the future day;

Yet sometimes the sunlight streameth,
  Over all that solemn road,
'Till its glory casts a halo
  On the soul's cast-off abode.

And, oh! then these spirit whispers
  That have borrowed earthly tones,
Swell to such floods of music,
  As high heaven only owns!

SWAYING and swimming through sunset air,
Insect wings shivering everywhere,
Shake out a song from these quivering wings,
Which a dreamy sense of their blessedness brings ;
How they joy in a being scarce measured by hours,
Since they die when the dewdrops come down on the
    flowers.
             Beautiful life !

Down in the quiet pools sheltered and deep,
In their silvery mail do the fishes sleep ;
Or up through the ripples they flash in the light,
Like a meteor's flame in a cloudless night ;
Soulless, and sinless, and fearless are they,
While they revel in life as it passes away.
             Beautiful life !

Cloudward and skyward upspringing, the birds
Pour over earth their musical words ;
They rain down their music from out of the sky,
And from every thicket and brookside sigh ;
As free as the songs of the waves of the sea,
Out pour their carols of rapturous glee !
             Beautiful life !

Out from each shadowy cavernous glen,
Out from each meadow and marsh and fen,

Out from the prairie and down from the hill,
Come cries of the life blest, low toned and shrill;
From everything living, and everywhere,
Gushes life's joyfulness filling the air!
Beautiful life!

And human life silvered with morning light,
Golden with noon, or flushing toward night;
Grand with its conflicts of tempest and storm,
In its every hour and every form;
Mellowed and deep in its growing old,
How can its riches be fully told?
Beautiful life!

PHANTOM BUILDING.

A FOOTSTEP in the dust we trace,
  And then, of him whose step was there,
We build above that lowly place,
  A phantom figure in the air.

Lone Crusoe saw a shadow host,
  Hold savage orgies on the strand,
Because upon that barren coast,
  A human footstep pressed the sand.

The Arab bites his wordless lip,
  To see an armèd train pass by,
When nought of barb or " desert ship,"
  Save footprints, meets his searching eye.

We see a dead stalk on a wall,
  And suddenly to golden bloom,
There bursts through all its death-spell's thrall,
  The wallflower's phantom o'er its tomb,

A snowless winter's walk we take,
  Through some deserted graveyard old,
Where 'neath our feet the scentless brake,
  And grass, lie withered, brown and cold.

Their rustling crush recals their past,
  Like magic life-word to them spoke,

8*

Their brown arms up toward Heaven they cast,
Their wintry doom of thraldom broke.

Up from the dull and frozen mould,
Transfigured springs the fragrant fern,
And verdant grass, and daisies bold,
Smile round each solemn gravestone's urn.

We pass—some trailing brambles clasp
Fast to our skirts with hookèd thorn ;
We stoop to loose this tightening grasp
Of stems, of life and verdure shorn.

We cast the rough encumbrance down,
When full-leaved up before us rise,
With berries bowed these briers brown,
Grown green and strong before our eyes !

Can summer skies melt bonds of death,
With surer skill than this we share ?
Dare magic words, in whispered breath,
Evoke more phantoms than *we* dare ?

What matter for the driving storms,
The drifting snows, life's wintrier parts,
When in *us* live all glowing forms,
Creative summer in our hearts ?

WHEN morning broke bright o'er the darkness that
  shrouded
The sleep-shackled world in a mantle of night,
When the wild wind had chased the dun vapor that
  clouded
The blue deep of æther obscuring its light,
When no prison confined, and no walls were around
  thee,
Hast thou never then felt that thou wast not yet free,
That the bondage of custom so closely had bound thee,
That other men's thoughts are a prison to thee?

Hast thou never grown sick in thy spirit with fearing
The laugh of some worm crept up higher than thou?
Or some pitiful fool, who had borrowed his sneering,
To whose broadcloth and gold all the multitude bow?
Yet thou dared not turn back, and with pride answer
  pride,
And with scorn spurn the scorn that fell heavy on thee?
Thy locks have been shorn, and thy hands have been
  tied,
False customs have bound thee! thou canst not be free!

Burst forth from thy bondage, proud spirit, and utter
Those truths that shall set other souls in a glow,
Let the lightning-bolt strike ere the deep thunders mutter,
Be free first thyself—then help all to be so!

Is not thy soul human, and life everlasting
A heritage free—by thy birthright thy own?
Who heirs an estate thine in grandeur surpassing,
Or who has a less, that thou ever hast known?

The laborer crushed in the dust shall awaken
From the sleep where he lost his dread portion of toil;
And the king shall leave earth when death's sceptre shall
    beckon,
Then the slave shall be peer of the lord of the soil!
No more shall the lordling in luxury silken,
Use the labor in which he has taken no part,
No more shall grieved echo sob back from the welkin
The sigh of the starved in mind, body, and heart.

For the grave owns but equals in dust it is 'tombing,
And souls find but equals beyond the dim shore,
Whose dark shrouding shadows, forbidding, lie glooming
Around death's deep waters we all must pass o'er.
Must the soul then, forgetting its own mighty powers,
Supine in the dust, put its birthright away,
Till the grim King of Terrors shall roll round the hours
To close up life's wintry and wearisome day?

Or shall it stretch forth its free wings, ere the dawning
Of life in the realms of the beautiful sky,
To meet the slow-coming, yet glorious morning,
Whose steps are approaching, whose advent is nigh?
When hand clasped in hand shall acknowledge its brother,
When peasant and prince shall be titles unknown,
When none shall claim rights he denies to another,
And all bow to one Monarch—one Father—one throne.

THE PICTURE ON THE WALL.

THERE's a soft dreamy landscape that hangs on the wall,
  Through the sweet Sabbath solitude whispering things,
That a single light footstep in parlor or hall,
  Would drown with the echoes each footstep brings.

Some artist unknown with his soul all aglow,
  With a light other eyes had no power to see,
And a heart whose deep poetry could not o'erflow,
  For words were denied and his spirit not free ;

Has here slowly evolved thro' his beautiful art,
  A shadowy scene from the dreamland within,
Where clouds shade that glory that poured on his heart,
  And his toil has brought twilight to soften its beam.

But thro' that soft light that glows dim on the lake,
  With its tinge on the foam and the archway grey,
On that brown ancient tower and tufted brake,
  And those clouds' ragged masses far floating away,

I can trace the pale glory of that spirit light,
  That but glowed for the soul of the poet alone,
And thro' those still shadows, foreboding the night,
  Are his fetters of soul to my spirit made known.

This glory and shadow so wedded in one,
  Give birth to a host of whispering dreams,

Who make silence their voice when they find us alone,
  To reveal the deep source of each life's hidden streams.

The landscape is lovely and brings to our view,
  The castles and rocks of some far away place,
But it shows us more faithfully, life-like, and true,
  The artist who painted those scenes which he traced.

I'VE been out in the " grand old woods " to-day,
  Where the earlier plant stems the damp earth part,
As their long chilled pulses begin to play,
  And their leaves toward the genial sunlight start;
Spring's first birds chirped on each budding tree,
  And merrily swung on each wind-swept bough,
And I never was younger, it seems to me,
  Or more of a child, than I am just now!

The frogs that were piping so shrill in the flood,
  Told the stories so oft in my hearing erst told,
And strangers were with me, the kind and the good,
  Who sang me the songs I had loved of old;
These spells have been breaking the chain-links of years,
  And sweeping me back to life's by-gone day,
Till my soul has swelled with its old time fears,
  Its loves and its joys that have passed away.

The fountains deep hid in my heart have gushed o'er,
  In tears of warm tenderness, spite of my will,
And I long for some dear one, familiar of yore,
  To catch its outpourings—its throbbings to still.
The kindness of strangers is touching and sweet,
  And gentle new friends for my gratitude call,
But I'd give all the world, this bright eve, but to meet,
  Some old friend I love—'twould be worth more than all!

BY A LAKE SIDE.

Night's dusky plumes float slowly over,
　From the cold grey eastern sky,
Toward where eve's bright pinions hover,
　Lingering ere the day shall die,
And leave the chambers of the west,
　To this still, solemn, starlit guest.

Flaming chariot wheels of glory,
　Such as bore the seer away,
Blazed beyond the lake before me,
　As they carried off the day;
Then as the fading splendor fled,
　Night's dreamy spells were round me shed.

Across the lake and land and river,
　Those witching spells my vision bear,
Till with joy's quick, sudden shiver,
　Meet I one remembered there:
Yon blue horizon lost the key,
That locked the absent one from me!

O! bless thee, Night! for power given,
　To melt such weary leagues away,
And keep, where'er life's bark be driven,
　Oblivion's ghostly shade at bay,
Till those once near us seem so yet,
And we forget we can forget!

THE DEATH WATCH.

Night had spread o'er earth's surface,
　A damp and darksome pall,
Ocean sent up its vapors,
　To overshadow all;
Silence had hushed sound's voices,
　All save the night-bird's call;
The dull monotonous murmur,
　Of wind and waterfall,
The cricket's chirp, and death-watch ticking,
　Ticking in the hollow wall.

On the couch sleep had deserted,
　Tossed the restless to and fro,
Listened to the lonely night-wind,
　Wished for morning's rosy glow.
Wearied of the wind's low murmur,
　And the stream's unceasing flow,
Tried to marshal into order,
　Thoughts that from confusion grow;
Turned and sighed for gifts that mortals,
　On earth are destined not to know,
Then held the breath and stilled heart-beating,
　To hear the death-watch ticking slow;
Ticking in the wall at midnight,
　Monotonous and low,
A keeping time to death's sure footsteps,
　'Mid summer's bloom and winter's snow.

Then slowly creeps a shivering shudder,
   Through each limb and nerve and bone,
A thrill of half delicious terror,
   Exquisitely lone,
That amid the day's broad beaming
   We would blush to own,
But now with darkness round us brooding,
   Fear's dark power is known,
Superstition grasps our heart-strings,
   And makes the mind its throne ;
And we think of hoarse death rattles,
   And the dying groan,
When we hear the death-watch ticking,
   Ticking in a gentle tone,
In the hollow wall at midnight,
   When we are alone.

AFAR across the billows' sounding roar—
The sky-like waters, and their star-like isles—
Why seeks the trav'ler on Italia's shore,
  'Mid clang of war, or old Rome's treach'rous wiles,
To find a land where genial nature smiles?
  Why search 'mid relics of forgotten art,
Where nature's tapestry drapes its ruined piles,
  For food to nourish in the mind and heart,
The latent feelings and the thoughts that may to being
      start?

Do Greece's statues to her noble sons,.
  Who died in exile by decrees unjust,
Teach him to love his own land's honored ones
  Who lie unsculptured, mould'ring back to dust?
Do gods of stone teach him a holier trust
  In him whom hands have never shadowed forth?
Or crumbling thrones or monarch's trampled bust,
  Instruct his heart how little strength is worth,
More than the prostrate forest kings in lands that gave
      him birth?

Do nameless cities 'mid the desert lands—
  Once royal seats, but now the bats' abode—
Tell that lone pilgrim wandering o'er the sands,
  One tale untaught by any woodland road.
The schoolboy from his father's house once trod?
  When solemn awe his youthful soul o'ercame,

Where the green light thro' matted branches showed
   The narrow path,—his pent breath scarcely came,
Lest he should wake some monster wild, or shape with-
   out a name.

As in his mantle 'neath the open sky,
   He counts the islets in the upper deep,
Does not the jackal's ever wakeful cry,
   Or hoarse hyena, banishing his sleep,
Remind him of those days, when 'mid his sheep,
   His father's dog kept hungry wolves at bay,
When their long howls and many pattering feet
   Wore the dull hours of tedious night away,
'Till o'er that lonely wilderness the morn rose pale and
   grey ?

The present danger melts and fades away,
   As mist wreaths vanish in the æther free;
For thro' the past his wakened mem'ries stray,
   His thoughts are busy far beyond the sea,
Where no red sands have buried bud and tree,
   And plain, and city 'neath their scorching waves,
Where wildbirds sing, where hums the honey bee ;
   And many a wildfowl its soft plumage laves,
In glassy lake and river deep, hoarse rushing from its
   caves ;

Or stream that gathers from each silvery rill,
   That winds through glen and narrow, dark ravine ;
An added item its deep course to fill,
   While trackless wildwoods raise their trunks between,

And bathe their feet amid the waters' sheen,
   And nod above the brink of each cascade,
Each leaning unto each its forehead green,
   To watch the motion of the flickering shade,
That their crossed arms, in airy dance, with the soft
    wind have made.

He fancies how that cabin, bare and rude,
   Might spread a shelter o'er his sleeping head,
Where beasts that prowl that houseless solitude,
   Awed by man's presence, would not dare to tread ;
An Indian wigwam, or a hunter's shed,
   Were safe protection in that lonely place,
Where nations once in mutual struggle bled,
   Dreaming of glory, yet have left no trace
Of nation or of tribe—no name of chieftain or of race.

Here all alone, from feud and faction free,
   " The world forgetting—by the world forgot"—
The forest lord beneath some sheltering tree,
   Might search as deeply in the mines of thought
As he whose brain 'mid foreign scenes had wrought,
   For gems of truth, where, 'mid his weary toil,
The very wild beast's desert howlings brought
   Back to his memory all the golden spoil
Of mental wealth he'd left unreaped upon his native soil.

By distance hallowed come the scenes of home—
   The rocky girdle of the ocean's surge—
The mountain's peak, the rushing cataract's foam,
   The tempest's shriek, the low wind's wailing dirge ;

The arrowy prows, that swift as wild wings urge
  Their trackless way across the swelling floods,
Caves that yawn o'er leagues of wonders huge,
  And over all the endless solitudes
Of forests wide and dim—his own land's dark old woods!

COME, beautiful snow, and bury the world,
It is foul with many a stain ;
And I long for a little while to look,
And behold it clean again !

Restlessly heaving to and fro,
Earth's millions turn and toil,
And lives are worn and traded away
For a foothold on God's soil.

For the body's bread and its clothes,
Its dwelling and burial place,
The soul is forgotten and thrown away,
And leaves but dust in its place.

Evil is cruel, and fierce, and strong,
And stealing the name of law,
Sends love to the gibbet and truth to jail,
And the human to market like straw.

My soul rebels with a fierce revolt,
But they bid it to bear the ill,
For a woman's sense of right they say,
Must wait on another's will.

They bind the hands and gag free lips,
And mock the exceeding pain ;
Oh ! the earth is foul ! thanks, beautiful snow,
For making it clean again !

I LOVE thee, Martha, with a love that liveth,
    With my deep passion for all lovely things,
Yet with that sad misgiving that receiveth,
    From ceaseless changes its melancholy tinge.
Love is our life—Earth's beauty—Heaven's brightness—
    The soul's responding to another's call;
The mountain's strength, the cloud-wing's fairy light-
      ness,
    The psalm of waves, of wind, and waterfall—
Wake in our hearts that restless sweet emotion,
    That gusheth upward toward the bright and true,
Even as rise the billowy tides of Ocean,
    When Dian beckons from the empyrean blue.
But when a true heart, in its ceaseless beating,
    Throbs out warm comfort to those lingering near,
Though in a crowd it give its passing greeting,
    The warmth it giveth makes that true one dear!

Day, crowned with sunbeams, sinks to rest,
   Pillowed 'mid clouds that blush and glow,
Transfigured by their royal guest
   From dun to rosy gold and snow.
The hand of evening comes to write,
   In shadowy letters on our wall,
Weird promise that the mist-veiled night
   On day's broad realm awaits to fall.

Yet ere that spell-enchanted light—
   That strange green light of summer eves,
That comes before the fire-flies light
   Their lamps among the whispering leaves—
Comes with its vague things half revealed,
   Like memories that we can't recall,
That tempt pursuit, but only yield
   An echo's answer to our call—
Let us put by each day-worn thought,
   And, in this Sabbath of the hours,
Wait for the good so often sought,
   So seldom found 'mong " human flowers."

That wisdom schoolmen have not learned,
   That deep-read sages oft deny—
By churchmen laughed to scorn, or spurned,
   Or passed in heedless silence by,
And yet which yearning spirits long,
   And hunger weary years to know,

9

Tho' sung in every wood-thrush song,
  And breathed thro' May woods' fragrant snow;
And this green forest twilight tells
  In sybil tones thro' dark-grouped trees,
One of the spirit's holiest spells,
  The key-note to its mysteries.

The heart in crowds which vainly sought
  Its secret pass-word answered back—
The one who learned what schoolmen taught
  To find, through his own soul, the track
By which those weird impressions come,
  Unasked, to haunt his thoughtful hours,
With visions of that Eden home
  The gypsies tell us once was ours—
Yet learned in vain; for through the soul
  No chart hath marked the devious way,
And, far as ever from the goal,
  He learned by turns to doubt and pray.
The one who sought for spirit lore,
  Of churchmen learned in creed and law,
Conning dry bones of dead faith o'er,
  Still doubting all its proofs he saw—
These might have learned, in this hushed wood,
  Alone with God and Nature's scroll,
In this still, solemn solitude,
  These untaught lessons of the soul.

Seek, delve and search, for wealth of gold,
  For knowledge of God's outward plan,
Toil for all learning, new and old,
  Make thought's rich spoil thine—if thou can;

But o'er the soul's entrenchments deep,
  No toil can bridge thy curious way;
To scale its ramparts, sheer and steep,
  In vain is art's or strength's essay;
For here, as by the Jordan's flood,
  Thy thought, like Israel's host, must stand:
Still the wild chafing of thy blood—
  Relax thy grasping, toil-stained hand—
Cool thy vexed spirit's feverish heat—
  Soothe down its each impulsive thrill—
Rest here, unshod, thy way-worn feet,
  Obedient to the words, "Stand still!"
Toil cannot win—gold cannot buy—
  Lore cannot give the soul its keys;
Itself sees not the seeing eye—
  Mind knows not mind's deep mysteries;
But like the glass reflecting back,
  The eye that seeks itself to see,
This twilight shows us what we lack,
  And what we are, and are to be.
And through the drifting mists that weave,
  Through warp of fact this woof of thought,
The waiting spirit can receive
  The truths its teachers have not taught,
And dimly as through distance far,
  Beholds its own deep secrets lie—
Or shadowy types of what they are,
  That vanish as they come more nigh.

And this is all—yet upward ever
  Those visions point us as they go,
Mute promise that past death's deep river
  Our souls shall learn themselves to know.

His spirit bears no weight of woe,
   Nor is it saddened by one pang ;
His heart beats no despairing throe,
   No storm-clouds o'er his spirit hang,
Nor dimming tear-drops fill his eyes,
To tell of grief or sad surprise.

Yet pleasure hath but little part
   In the dull chaos of his brain,
Mirth quickens not his sluggish heart,
   Which only knows it feels no pain—
For joy hath lost the glad control
With which it ruled his willing soul.

His stagnant thoughts in silence creep,
   Nor seek new mysteries to explore,
Unheeding as the rocks that sleep
   On grim oblivion's murky shore ;
Nor, but from habit, would they turn,
To where Heaven's watch-fires dimly burn.

The dormouse in its winter cell,
   Its death-like lethargy may break
In winter's wildest storm,
   As he from out this stupor wake,
While wintry circumstances hold
His spirit in their icy fold.

O, spring-time! hast thou lost thy way,
  And lingered in the sunnier bowers
Of hearts that catch each genial ray,
  To warm affection's springing flowers,
That thou hast left life's freezing chill,
Upon his wearied spirit still?

O, WHY that sad, murmuring, half-conscious strain,
"Be hushed my dark spirit!" sung over again?
Are there storms with their shadows cast over thy sky,
That thus thou should'st sing them their lullaby?
Do the vapors of cloud-land thy spirit enfold
As the dun mists of autumn their volume have rolled
Round the mountain that basked in the summer sun
Ere the hours of darkness and gloom had come?
Or in that strain is there lingering still
Tones that no more thy soul shall thrill—
Echoes of voices that far through the past,
The bewildering spell of their melody cast—
That over, and over, and over again,
Dream-like and low, like the wind harp's strain,
"Be hushed my dark spirit!" seems ever to swell,
Unbidden from out of thy heart's deepest cell?

Is there dwelling a magic in sounds like these,
Which, faint like the voice of the dying breeze,
Comes over the heart in its loneliest hour,
And soothes it to rest with its quiet power?
The weary heart bowed with its burden stills,
As that mournful sound through its chambers thrills—
Stills from its throbbing tempestuous pain,
To list to that sad sound o'er again;
For weary and sad tho' the spirit be
It echoes the voices of memory.

SHEAVES OF TIME'S HARVEST.

TIME passed his hand o'er the brow of youth,
And ploughed deep furrows where once 'twas smooth,
Then he wrote great lines of thought and care
In the place of the smiles that it used to wear;
Then sprinkled the ebon locks with grey,
And faded the light of the eyes away,
And the reaper smiled at the mourners' grief,
As he gathered home this ripened sheaf.

Time stood by a forest dim and old,
As its thousand years were well nigh told,
And its fallen kings lay mouldering there,
Where the grey moss swung in the chilly air,
From ocean to ocean's distant shore
That trackless forest shadowed o'er;
But a nation toils where those wild-wood leaves
Were garnered once with that reaper's sheaves.

Time stood on Baalbec's giant walls,
And paced thro' proud Palmyra's halls,
And like the echo of his tread
Came funereal wailings for the dead;
And now the desert blasts alone
Sigh o'er each fallen monarch's throne—
The only spirit abroad that grieves
Over those long since gathered sheaves.

Time leaned against the humble shed,
That sheltered the starving peasant's head,

And though heart-strings broke as the root fell in,
The groans of the dying were drowned in the din.
What recked old Time the peasant's woes?
He had looked on a dying nation's throes!
Alike to him man's joy or grief,
As he gathers one more human sheaf.

Yet waiteth not that reaper dread,
For the flower to wither and droop its head,
For he cuts with his sickle, sharp and keen,
The golden ear and the leaflet green,
The babe that sports at its grandsire's knee,
And the grey old man alike takes he,
The starting bud and the withered leaf,
He gathers to add to his well-grown sheaf.

The rose-tinged petals together rolled,
And the bud untwisting each fragrant fold,
The flower on its stem, scarce fully blown,
He bears with his sheaves to his harvest home;
The youthful while hope still paints on the air,
Visions of glory enchantingly fair,
The reaper gathers, nor heeds our grief,
He has need, perhaps, of this blooming sheaf.

Alone that silent reaper stands
As he binds his sheaves with his bony hands,
And he scans the field of his harvest o'er
As he scanned it a thousand years before—
And he laughs as he watches the puny toil
Of those whose labors he makes his spoil,
For the world and its creatures, like Autumn leaves,
He binds together—Time's harvest sheaves.

Christmas Eve, 1855.

I CALL thee! Dost thou hear my call?
Or have those thrilling inner chords
Become too dull, and still, and cold,
  To vibrate to my words?
Within that chamber of thy heart
  Where old things half forgotten lie,
By dust and cobwebs wreathed and veiled,
  Comes no fresh life to memory?
Stirs not within that silent fane,
  Some pulse of life lived once before,
When well-known hands unbar its gates,
  And well-known footsteps cross its floor?
Send back those walls no echo note,
  To sounds that break their holy hush,
When once they pealed an answer back,
  To every wayward music gush?
Within that temple's inmost shrine,
  Will memory's statue breathe no more,
Like Memnon's, those deep anthem tones,
  It chanted oft in days of yore?

There is a charm to break its sleep,
  (Would I could wake that magic spell)
When gathering its long silent voice,
  Loud, deep, and long, its tones shall swell;
9*

But till its long appointed hour
   Slow wheels around it must sleep on,
And though I rouse an echo's voice,
   I cannot wake one *living* tone.
I enter that deserted room,
   My garments brush the dust away,
One quenchless votive lamp burns on,
   To light my dim and dusky way;
Feels not that pallid statue's brow,
   The living hand upon it pressed?
Does it not feel the holly wreath,
   I bring to crown its silent rest?

I have been with thee—but I turn,
   And bolt and bar that temple's door;
And know not if one life thrill told
   Thy soul my shadow crossed its floor!

ANNIVERSARY LETTER.

CONDERSPORT, *Christmas Eve*, 1856.

I ONCE had a friend, who hath passed away,
Like the morning mists of a summer's day :
Forth like an anchorless barque he went,
But I know not whither his footsteps bent.
Is he wearily climbing the pathway of fame,
To hear echo mockingly shouting his name ?
Is there glowing around him the sunshine of home,
Or treads he the " valley of shadows" alone ?
'Neath a rainbow arch in the unknown land,
Enrol they his name in a white-winged band ?

But a shadow falls on me with a menace of woe,
Ah! his soul is yet fettered with earth-bonds I know,
For never yet did that shadow fall,
From a spirit released from its earthly thrall,
Nor, alas! from a soul with its sins forgiven,
Spreading its wings for its home in Heaven !

Ah! Soul of my Friend!   As the clouds in the sky,
Trail their shadows o'er all things beneath them that lie,
So the shade that cast over my spirit its chill,
Hath shown me thy soul is enclouded still !

But hast thou no token but this one to-night ?
No message to speed like an " arrow of light,"
Athrill with thy feeling—aglow with thy thought ?

Oh! woe for the lessons that world-craft hath taught!
Oh, woe! if the love which hath taught thee the cause
Of every effect of God's wonderful laws,
Hath curtained thy innermost self from the light—
If reason hath blinded thy instinct's sight,
And deeper woe, if the dross of earth—
Things meaner, and less, and of poorer worth—
Have darkened thy soul with their daily care,
Till thou seest but their mildew everywhere!

LEXINGTON, ILL., *Christmas Eve,* 1857.

I HEAR the rush of mountain streams,
Underneath the evergreens,
    That bend beneath their load of snow;
I hear the north wind's echo call,
From mountain unto "mountain wall,"
    Where the dark pine woods grow.

I see the unfading mosses cling,
And hosts of yellow lichens spring,
    From leafless trunk, and fallen bough—
I see the green club-mosses creep,
Along the ferny ledges steep,
    As tho' I stood among them now!

The thousand miles that intervene,
Grow narrow as the pebbly stream,
    Before the homestead door;
And as night's deep'ning shadows darken,
I almost hold my breath to harken,
    To the footsteps on the floor;
And the old familiar call,
From the stairway in the hall,
    Sounds in my ear once more.

But I turn me slow away,
From the flickering lights that play,
    On the cottage window bars,

And a mist obscures my sight—
I may not pass home's door to-night—
  So reads the fiat of the stars.

Ah me! 'Tis Christmas Eve again,
And it belongs not unto them,
  But is like a monumental stone,
  Sacred to memory of one,
Passed and gone—I know not whither—
For a time—perhaps for ever!

'Tis Christmas Eve! I sigh with pain,
  For old Time's kaleidoscope
  Has not answered last year's hope—
Has not returned the lost again—
  Nor given me the faintest trace,
  Of the lost one's hiding place;
And these lines I now indite,
  By thy eyes may ne'er be read,
For I know not if I write,
  To the living or the dead.

But whether in the quick warm flesh,
  Or in robes that angels wear—
Whether 'mid old scenes or 'mid fresh—
  Or full of joy, or full of care—
If on a scaffold or a throne,
  Or if released from earthly thrall,
Thou hast learned 'mid stars to roam,
And claim yon over-arching dome
For ever as thy glorious home—

I ask not; while the snow flakes fall,
Upon the hills we used to tread,
   Upon this evening I will call
On thee, if living—or if dead!

There! good night! God's blessing on thee!
   Blessed dreams attend thy sleep;
If in Heaven, may angels crown thee,
   And waft thee to an upper deep!

THEY say that the elves are dead and gone,
　　And that never more by hill or lea,
Will the fairy rings in the grass be worn,
　　By the nightly dance as they used to be.

The frost may blight, and the drouth may burn,
　　And the grasshopper harvest the hay,
No more will you charge it to witch or elf,
　　Since their games have had their day.

Believe it not! They are living still!
　　You can find their traces night by night,
Where they spread a thousand gossamer webs,
　　About in the dew to bleach them white.

They are spread like veils all over the grass,
　　And over the drowsy red clover heads,
White nettings of mist, with a wealth of pearls,
　　That are strung like beads on the shining threads.

Go, rob from the fairy bleaching ground,
　　A veil to shadow some beaming face—
The pearls dissolve, and a knotted string,
　　Of that fairy web is the only trace!

Ay! watch for the elves! They are living still!
　　But go to the haunts where they love to go,

Where the red moss chalices left behind,
Are telling of last night's nectar flow!

Await them in faith! await them in love!
When the young moon's boat sails down the west,
And the blessings they leave in the woods and fields,
Will linger around you and make you blest!

The winds may give the treasures back,
  They gather from the dewy flowers,
Leaving along their fragrant track,
  Sweet perfumes from Arcadian bowers.

The waters may return the bread,
  The liberal hand upon it cast,
But when will Time's returning tread,
  Bring back the dead, the buried past?

Morn may restore those glowing hues,
  That evening's curtain wrapped in shade,
And evening shed again those dews,
  That morning dried from wood and glade.

But Memory with oft wearied feet,
  Must wander o'er past scenes in vain,
For never from their dark retreat,
  Will bygone hours return again!

A STUDENT marks each moment as it passes,
 By the slow droppings from the eaves,
Pattering on the broken, rustling grasses,
 And the dock's red-spotted leaves.

Then out so solemnly and slowly,
 The drops the precious moments dole,
That the dim night hours, calm and holy,
 Seem endless to that watching soul.

While day gathereth fresh splendor,
 In the caves of eastern seas,
Earnest night, so calm and tender,
 Locks sleep's gates with silence' keys.

But past their portals ere their closing,
 A horde of spirits had entered in,
That 'mid the body's sweet reposing,
 Their pranks upon the soul begin.

Hope, who cheered thro' day's hard battle,
 Queens it now on reason's throne,
The real's work day toil and rattle,
 Merged in a music all her own.

Or dreaming Faith o'erleaps for ever,
 Forgetful of life's parting pain,

That deeply shadowed, silent river,
  Once crossed, which ne'er is crossed again.

Or stricken grief, with icy fingers,
  On the heart's bare quivering chords,
Plays wailing music such as lingers,
  In love's despairing, farewell words.

But oftener fancies fast and fleeting,
  Wild revels hold in every dream,
Like troops of summer lightnings meeting,
  Kindred flashes in each stream.

So pass the night hours with the sleeping,
  But without the gates of rest,
Unwilling, weary vigils keeping,
  Sits wakeful thought's unsleeping guest.

Then that student still and lonely,
  Learns of voiceless Night and Thought,
For in the deepest silence only,
  Their higher miracles are wrought

On the beating pulse of nature,
  Lays each witch her finger light,
Revealing by that secret feature,
  Every heart-throb hid from sight.

It is worth this watch unsleeping,
  With the rain-song in one's ear,
Thus to gather to one's keeping,
  Earnest truths taught only here!

THANK God! I'll be a child no more!
   Life's earlier woes and fears are dead,
I've trod upon youth's utmost shore,
And life full grown is half way o'er,
   With all its storms and darkness fled.

My morning dawn was dark and wild,
   But cheery grows the lengthening day,
And since I've ceased to be a child,
The genial skies have ever smiled,
   And now I love its lingering way.

Two brimful cups life offered me,
   A cup of joy—a cup of care—
My right hand grasped the draught of glee—
The left thrust care's grim bowl from me—
   And life has since grown rich and fair!

It may be dangers all unseen,
   Have lain in wait about my path—
It may be pitfalls lay between
My footsteps in the path I've been;
   What matter? I have passed unscathed.

It may be down the hidden slope,
   My restless feet must soon descend,
I must with fiercer dangers cope—
I will not fear, but go in hope,
   And trust in the Unfailing Friend!

ALL the woods are full of blossoms,
It is now the Moon of Blossoms,
The Moon of all the snow white flowers.*
The May cherry has departed,
Swung its feathery plumes of sweetness
For awhile on every wind breath,
On the slender twigs that bore them ;
Then upon the breeze that kissed it
Strewed the snow flakes of its petals.
  The wild plum had shed its sweetness,
Till the air was laden with it ;
Till the drowsy air grew drunken
With the fragrance of its blooming.
Then the blossoms blushed with pleasure—
Blushed to find themselves more fragrant
Than all other early flowers.
  And the wild bees from the torpor,
Of the long and idle winter,
Waked to work amid the flowers.
Then from out the leafless snowdrift,
From the plum-tree's blushing snowdrift,
Came the busy hum of labor,
Came the happy song of labor,
Mingled with the drowsy odor
Of its own exceeding sweetness :
Till its petals withered slowly,

ᵏ The Senecas call May the Moon of White Blossoms.

Shrunk and shrivelled in the sunshine.
They refused to leave the calyx,
And go drifting in their beauty,
Like the apple's faded petals;
Like the graceful snow flakes drifting
In the passing winds that shook them.
Then the woods ablaze with purple,
Flushed and flamed in all their borders.
Crimson fringes edged the prairies,
Rosy purple framed the rivers
With a setting richer, rarer,
Than the costliest palace mirrors,
Though the lowliest and poorest
With their seedy rags unchidden,
And their bare feet unforbidden,
Might adjust their shaggy tresses
By those grand and wondrous mirrors;
And the children gathered treasures,
Priceless treasures, from the tree-tops,
In those countless purple branches,
In the pea-bloom of the red bud.
But before this flushing fadeth,
Comes the dog-wood's robes of whiteness,
Mingled with this royal raiment,
And from out each clump and thicket,
And from every patch of brushwood,
From beside the pools of water,
From the hillock and the sand-ridge,
And from out the isles of timber,
And the borders of the prairie,
Comes a fragrance fresher, sweeter,
Than the breath of strawberries,

Than the odor of the roses;
Like the smell of fruit and flowers,
With a fairy's blessing on it,
Making it a thing unreal,
Only something we have dreamed of,
Though it freshens all the senses
With its penetrating presence.
'Tis the fragrance of the crabtree,
'Tis the bursting of the flowers,
From the rosy buds, that swelling
With the prisoned odors in them,
Could not longer hold their riches.

And the earth is strewed with blossoms,
Blue as is the sky above it.
Blue-bells blossom by the water,
May-bells bloom among the grasses,
The wild larkspur seeks the road-side,
And the blue phlox everywhere
Utters forth its soul in odor.

And like stars amid the azure
Early buttercups are blooming;
And this bursting world of flowers,
Keeping time to all the trilling,
Sinking, swelling songs and carols,
Of the whip-poor-wills and robins,
Swing and sway upon the breezes,
In the airy dance of flowers,
In the white-robed Moon of Blossoms.

A CLOUD o'ershadoweth my soul,
With many a silvery purple fold,
And ragged edge of hazy gold,
And sunset smiling through the whole.

A shadow, in whose softening shade,
The long-ago comes floating back,
With song and perfume on its track,
And seems as 'twere the present made.

The far-off, through the wilds of space,
A welcome vision draweth near,
Wreathed with familiar smiles, and dear,
To me in this lone stranger place.

The future, in a misty veil,
Draws this magic cloud beneath,
Like Dian in a vapory wreath,
And tells her prophet tale.

I seem to leave this mould of clay,
And out among these things of thought,
So near me by enchantment brought,
To go, ethereal as they.

10

I thank thee, cloud, that thou hast made
Amid life's toils, so stern and real,
An hour so tender and ideal
As this, of light embalmed in shade.

I thank thee, that the glare of day
Sometimes dissolves in clouds like this;
Where rainbow prophecies of bliss,
Shine on my often darkened way.

WE meet as the waters meet,
  Our souls together run,
  And mingle into one,
And life grows deep and sweet.
  From the heart that beats in thee
  Stirs the inmost pulse in me,
And the thought that in my brain,
  Struggles faintly to be said,
Thy soul echoes back again,
  Ere a sentence has been made.
We quicken each the other's thought,
  But so akin our sayings rise,
  That be they vain, or be they wise,
·Which spoke them we remember not.

The streams of our lives diverge, and change,
  And labor attends us whither we go ;
New events and faces, diverse and strange,
  Drift around us, wavering to and fro ;
And each hath its load of especial care,
And a different tide, a different air,
  Is urging us evermore on and on.
But we meet again, as the waters meet,
  And the past is vanished away and gone ;
And now life has grown—oh, more than sweet!

The treasures we've gathered, the lives we've led,
Have deepened and widened the heart and head;
And yet, ever tendeth my soul to thee—
And ever thy spirit is coming to me,
As the rivers tend down to their home in the sea!

THE END.